T0032440

E L BLOCK

AMERICAN GOTHIC

AMERICAN
GOTHIC

TitleTown Publishing, LLC
P.O. Box 12093 Green Bay, WI 54307-12093
920.737.8051 | titletownpublishing.com

Designer: Euan Monaghan
Editor: Tracy C. Ertl
Proofreader: Megan Richard

PUBLISHER'S CATALOGING-IN-PUBLICATION DATA:

Names: Block, E L, author.

Title: American Gothic / E L Block.

Description: Green Bay, WI : TitleTown Publishing, LLC, [2022]

Identifiers: ISBN: 978-1-955047-04-3 (paperback)
              978-1-955047-05-0 (eBook)

Subjects: LCSH: American Dream--Fiction. | Success--Fiction. | Man-woman relationships--Fiction. | Interpersonal relations--Fiction. | Paranormal fiction. | Suspense fiction. | Psychological fiction. | LCGFT: Thrillers (Fiction) | BISAC: FICTION / Thrillers / Supernatural. | FICTION / Ghost. | FICTION / Gothic.

Classification: LCC: PS3602.L64263 A44 2022 | DDC: 813.6--dc23

For my family and friends.
Thank you for believing in me.

Contents

"August came, and with it already a faint and troubling premonition of the autumn – a breath, a fragrance, and an odor – that somehow spoke of summer's ending."

–Thomas Wolfe
American Author

High School

I fell in love with Adam Shepherd at summer camp. In Essex County, the public and parochial students were adversaries, but at Camp Laurelwood, we were one in the same. The kids from Essex. I didn't care for sports or games, and wanted nothing to do with the water, but I loved watching Adam enjoy them. At the end of every school year, I looked forward to seeing how he'd changed since the summer before. *Would he be taller? Would he have braces now? Would his hair be different?* I learned everything I could about him, and he didn't even know my name. Once we aged out of the summer camp program, I was lucky if I saw Adam from a distance a few times each year. The summer before my junior year, it was announced that the parochial high school was being shut down due to faltering attendance, and its remaining students would be integrated with the public high school. Fate was finally bringing us together, but it would still be an entire school year before Adam Shepherd knew my name.

I often lingered in the empty halls after creative writing club, just to get a glimpse of him coming in from football practice. He always looked at me and smiled, but I knew it didn't mean anything. Adam smiled at everyone.

He was good looking, popular, on the honor roll, the quarterback of the football team, and the lead in the school play. Everyone adored him. He had a beautiful girlfriend, of course – Isabelle – but she had been transferred to a Catholic boarding school in Boston when the high schools were combined.

I'd never been one to join things. I did love creative writing club, not only because I loved literature, but because it was largely a silent and autonomous activity. That year I painted sets for the school play, I joined the photography club and the school newspaper – anything that kept me quietly behind the scenes, and gave me a reason to be wherever Adam was. My best friend, Amy, begrudgingly joined them all with me. I was the only friend she had, and going along with whatever I was doing always beat the alternative of being by herself. There was something about Adam I was just so drawn to, even without knowing him personally. After a year of being nearer to him than ever before, I was no longer content to be silently observing his world from the sidelines. It was time to become a part of it.

The summer before senior year, I was allowed to take the train by myself for the first time, to visit my older sister, Katherine, in New York. She was enrolled in a summer internship program at Columbia University, where she studied architecture. Kate had always been beautiful, smart, and popular. She never had an awkward stage, an embarrassing moment, or so much as a bad hair day. It was truly unfair. We had all the same facial features, the same body type, even similar voices...but somehow, Kate was beautiful, and I was not. I was as mousey as they came. If I was going to take a real step into Adam's world senior year, that needed to change.

We walked to the Starbucks at the edge of the Columbia campus, and I told Kate all about him. She was surprised to hear me talk so incessantly, and with such passion, about anything other than books or coffee. "The boyfriend market is basically like the housing market," she told me. "Everyone wants the ideal house, in the ideal location, at the ideal price – but you only realistically get two of the three. The cute nice guys aren't usually smart, the smart nice guys aren't usually cute, and the cute smart guys aren't usually nice." Adam was a rare trifecta. I needed to be a rare trifecta, too. Kate was more than excited to help, insisting I was already everything I thought I wasn't.

That night we sat down on the sofa in the living area of Kate's tiny, one room apartment and we watched an old Audrey Hepburn movie called *Sabrina*. I could really relate to Sabrina Fairchild. She'd been in love with David Larrabee her entire life, and he didn't even know her name. She went away for two years, to culinary school in France, I think, and came back a beautiful, sophisticated woman that he was instantly drawn to. That was exactly what I needed to do, but I had two months, not two years.

Kate loaned me some of her clothes, and taught me how to dress in a way that flattered my figure, versus catering to the current trend. Let's be honest, no matter what decade it was when you were in high school, no current trend was ever really that flattering. Our mother used to take us shopping for new school clothes in New York City every late summer. I can still picture her walking down the street with one of her long, skinny cigarettes between her fingers, pointing at the store windows in disgust as she saw what was back in fashion that year. The year bell bottoms re-emerged as fit and flare jeans, she needed a second glass of chardonnay at lunch just to get through the rest of the afternoon. Those shopping trips ended when Kate graduated. My mother had come to the conclusion that high-end boutiques were wasted on me. She also knew that she couldn't send me to the local mall on my own, because I'd return with one sweater (that looked almost exactly like a sweater I already had) and a half dozen new books.

Kate showed me how to apply a little makeup for a fresh and flawless look that wasn't overdone. Prior to that, my makeup routine was Clearasil and Chapstick. She showed me how to style my long, brown hair so that it had volume and shine without looking wet, teased, or product heavy. She knew exactly what would work for me, because she'd already done the legwork to figure out exactly what would work for her.

I was ready. This was the year Adam Shepherd would know my name – just as soon as I changed it. Betsy sounded too cute for a young woman, but Elizabeth seemed much too formal. I didn't care for Beth or Liz. And God forbid, Lizzie. That would make anyone on the entire Eastern seaboard think of Lizzie Borden.

Lizzie Borden took an axe,
And gave her mother forty whacks,
When she saw what she had done,
She gave her father forty-one.

Once again, Kate had it made. Kate was the perfect shortened name for Katherine. It was mature, but not old. It was strong and smart, but still feminine. Our mother always said that with a last name like Farmer, it was imperative we had the most sophisticated first names possible. I considered going by my middle name, Jane. Using my initials could be very literary, I thought, but E.J. Farmer didn't sound the least bit feminine or alluring. Elizabeth it would have to be.

Everyone took notice when I walked through the doors on the first day of school, not just because I looked different than before, but because I was no longer striving to go unnoticed. The most popular football players were gathered together in a group just outside the doors to the gym. The same handful of them were always huddled around one another, and always up to something stupid. Every one of them was looking at me, including Adam. He smiled as always, and for the first time ever, I looked him in the eyes and smiled back. They were so beautifully blue.

We had more classes together our senior year, and in every one, Adam seemed to choose the seat closest to mine. My favorite class was English, not just because I loved literature and language more than anything, but because Adam sat directly behind me. Every time the teacher gave a stack of handouts to each row, instructing us to take one and pass the rest back, I looked forward to that split second when the papers connected us. He always whispered "thank you" as he took the handouts from me, and every time I heard it, I could feel the apples of my cheeks become warm.

The creative writing club met in the English room right after school. The football players had just finished practice and were heading up the stairs from the locker room as I was walking out the back doors to head home. Adam caught up with me. "Hey, mind if I walk with you?"

I silently panicked. The first words I'd ever say to Adam Shepherd needed to be perfect. Also, I hadn't spoken to anyone in the last few hours, what if I needed to clear my throat and my first words to him came out gravelly and disgusting? The clock was ticking. I had to take the risk and speak before he decided I was rude and walked away forever. "Of course you can walk with me. Where's your Jeep?" *Phlegm free. Thank God.*

"Getting an oil change," he smiled. "I'll have it back tomorrow morning." He seemed relieved to hear such a kind reply. Most of the girls in school seemed to think you had to treat a guy poorly in order to gain his attention and keep his interest. Kate said that was only true of guys who were looking for a chase, and ultimately, a conquest. That wasn't Adam.

It was a beautiful, clear afternoon, without a cloud in the sky. It still looked and felt like summer, but the scent of the air told me that fall was just around the corner. Fall was my favorite season. Sweaters, boots, falling leaves, and pumpkin spice everything.

It was a homecoming.

The buses were filing out of the school parking lots and disbursing throughout Essex County. Paper boys rode up and down every street, reaching deep into the canvas bags slung over their shoulders, and whipping rolled-up evening papers onto one front porch after another. The sounds of talking, laughing, and singing along with the stereo grew louder and then softer again, as cars filled with students drove past us as we walked.

"I hope your girlfriend won't mind us walking home together." *Subtle, Elizabeth.*

"We broke up over the summer. Going to different schools last year was hard. Plus, she likes to party and drink, and that's not really my thing." The timing couldn't have been more perfect.

"That's too bad." *Lie.* "So, what is your thing?"

"Other than football, senior year is all about studying hard and getting into a great college. I want to be a doctor. My little sister is sick and, I don't know, I think I'd like to help sick people."

"Adam, that's really great."

"Thanks," he smiled. "What about you?"

"I've always dreamed of becoming a best-selling author, just like Margaret Fuller." We had already turned the corner onto my street, and I found myself wishing I lived miles and miles further from the school.

"Can I give future best-selling author, Elizabeth Farmer, a ride to school tomorrow?" Those might have been the greatest words ever strung together to form a question. Adam Shepherd knew my name, and hearing him say it removed any doubt that my given name had been perfect for me all along. "Sure, that would be great," I said casually, while screaming on the inside. I couldn't wait to call Kate and tell her that Adam Shepherd had just walked me home from school!

I was the envy of every girl in school when I climbed down from the passenger seat of Adam's Jeep in the student parking lot. "See you later," he smiled, as he headed in the opposite direction for first period. Every time I glanced at him in our common classes that day, he was looking at me, smiling. After school, he was waiting at my locker to take me home.

That was the start of everything.

Adam and I were inseparable all through our senior year. I went to every one of his football games. He read everything I wrote. We studied together almost every night, and spent hours talking about college and the future. That used to be Amy and I, but she seemed to disappear rather suddenly once Adam and I got together. We went to the homecoming dance, where we were crowned king and queen. We double dated with his friends, who had quickly become my friends. He brought me with him whenever he visited his little sister in the hospital. We took our SATs together.

I was the valedictorian of our graduating class. My father, Kate, and Adam were so proud of me. I think my mother was more pleased that I was homecoming queen. Our parents met for the first time after the graduation ceremony, and we took photos together in our caps and gowns. We made plans to move to New York City together over the summer, with a matching pair of acceptance letters to New York University in the fall. Adam was going to be an incredible doctor, and I was going to be a *New York Times* best-selling author, just like Margaret Fuller.

We were going to have it all.

College

Our freshman and sophomore years of college were better than anything I could've imagined, but then things took a major turn for the worse. Adam's little sister lost her battle with Leukemia, and his parents' marriage couldn't survive her death. They owed a small fortune in medical expenses, and now funeral and divorce expenses as well. Needless to say, they could no longer afford to pay the balance of Adam's tuition. He had a few scholarships and grants, which covered part of it, but we had to figure out how to make the rest ourselves. Spending the summer back at Camp Laurelwood as counselors gave us just enough spending cash to get through the school year, but it wasn't going to be nearly enough for this. Together we made the decision that I would take some time off from school and find a job, so that Adam could continue on. We agreed that once he graduated and started a medical residency, we would get married, then he would take over supporting us while I finished my literature degree.

New York City was beyond expensive. We moved into a big, old house just off campus right before our junior year began. Well, *his* junior year. There were eight of us sharing the four-bedroom, one-bathroom house, which made it a very affordable option. It was Adam, myself, and six of his med school classmates. I was the only girl. Of all the potential things there are to be scared of in a run-down hundred-year-old house, let me tell you, I would have preferred a good old-fashioned poltergeist to the unspeakable horrors of one bathroom shared with seven college guys. I was grateful to still be a part of college life, but once again, I was practically alone, silently observing Adam's world from the sidelines.

I was working at a campus bar called The Library. I hated it, but I was able to make far more money than I could working a retail job for not much more than minimum wage. I would walk back to the house just after bar close, which wasn't very smart with all the drunk guys hanging around near the campus. Despite being exhausted, I was rarely able to fall sleep, so I'd end up resting on the couch and watching home improvement shows. It reminded me of staying home sick as a kid, and constantly worrying about what I was missing at school. *Will I be terribly behind when I get back? Will the seating arrangement have changed? Will my friends have made new friends?* I'd usually crawl into bed just as Adam was getting up in the morning, reveling in the warmth of the space he left behind, and we'd talk a little bit while he got ready for his first class. It was the only part of the day I really got to spend with him.

Coffee was a godsend. It was cheap, it kept me going, and it killed my appetite, which was the closest thing I had to a fitness plan. How Adam went to class all day, studied all night, and still found time for a daily run, was beyond me. He never touched coffee, or alcohol for that matter. I envied his discipline, his good habits, and his unwavering optimism. He said that his patients would be more likely to trust him as their doctor if he was the embodiment of health and wellness.

I sat there with my cup of coffee every morning and watched everyone rush out the door to begin their day, feeling as though mine was already over. I studied every inch of the quiet house as I recovered from a long night of serving dollar beers and cheap rail mixers to the undergraduate masses. It had good bones, as they often said on the home improvement shows. High ceilings, hardwood floors, ornate detailing, and tall leaded-glass windows. She was a grand house, once, but she'd been worn down by years of mistreatment and lack of attention. This wasn't the life she was created for. Despite being inhabited, she was nothing more than a shell. Hollow and cold. Defeated. Walking around inside of her, alone, was like walking around inside of myself.

Our landlord was about as absentee as they came, so when I wasn't sleeping or working at the bar, I would make improvements to the house to keep myself busy and out of everyone's way. I found a lot of discarded furniture and building materials on curbs. I struck a deal with an art student who worked part-time at Sherwin Williams; I'd stretch and prime her canvases in exchange for free returned and mis-tinted paint. I even started a square foot garden, in the tiny greenspace between the house and the alley behind it. In a neighborhood full of run-down college housing, one grand old home had been relatively returned to her former glory, thanks to me. It was the only aspect of my life that gave me any sense of purpose or accomplishment, at the time. I could have been, and should have been, using that time to write. But I wasn't even keeping a journal anymore. My present reality was far too disappointing to commit to paper.

✟

One of New York University's most renowned literary professors, Susan Smith-Brown, added a brand new first-floor laundry room to her nearby brownstone. I knew this because I stalked her on social media. I was able to pick up her old washer and dryer on the university's buy/sell/trade site. I screwed some used casters onto an old wooden door that had been propped up against the outside of the house, and wheeled the washer and dryer right down the sidewalk in broad daylight, without an ounce of shame. The guys hauled them down to the basement, we connected them, and voila! No more expensive and crowded laundromats, or sneaking into the dormitory coin-ops after hours. I wanted so badly to be taking Susan Smith-Brown's American Literature course that semester. I'd been waiting two years to be eligible for it. But the closest I could get to her was doing my laundry in her old machines.

Part of me had naively hoped that after dropping a few smart literary references while acquiring the washer and dryer, Professor Smith-Brown would have taken notice of me. Maybe she'd offer me a position as her teaching assistant, or at the very least, she'd invite me for coffee and a walk through her favorite hole in the wall New York City bookstore. That didn't happen. I said hello to her at the campus farmer's market a few weeks later. She smiled and nodded in passing, without the slightest recollection that I was laundry cart girl. *God, I really needed someone to talk to.*

I often thought about Amy. I regretted not maintaining our friendship after Adam and I started dating. When I thought back to our senior year of high school, I couldn't recall seeing her once, not even at graduation. I was sure she was attending Columbia, that had always been her plan. I really wanted to know how she was doing, what she was reading, and if she was dating anyone. I missed the way we used to spend hours talking over coffee, never running out of interesting topics to discuss. I sent her a text every now and then, but she never responded. I couldn't really blame her. I'd been a terrible friend.

I was certain she had a new best friend by now, one who was much more interesting than I was. One who was much more dependable. There was a strange and sad relief to our friendship falling away, because Amy was no doubt busy achieving everything she ever said she would, while nothing at all was working out the way I'd carefully planned. She would most likely be very disappointed to learn that I had dropped out of college, was working in a dive bar, and didn't have enough left in me at the end of the day to read a book, let alone write one.

My Parents

I felt lost and frustrated, like I was wasting the best years of my life doing nothing worthwhile. This wasn't at all how things were supposed to go. I was a rare trifecta, for Christ's sake. In my daydreams, this time in my life was better than I'd ever imagined, leaving Essex County behind for the excitement of New York City. Adam and I were madly in love. I was Susan Smith-Brown's teaching assistant, and attending fancy dinners and cocktail parties where I rubbed elbows with New York's literary elite. I was Audrey Hepburn, radiating with charm, style, and grace. I was writing, and brilliantly.

One morning, I told Adam I was going to take the train home for an overnight visit with my parents. He was surprised, and quite frankly, so was I. I never thought I'd feel so misplaced, so disconnected from who I was, that I'd actually want to go home. Adam encouraged me to go, though I'm sure he was wondering if we could afford it. But that's what Adam did. He understood. He encouraged. He supported. No matter how exhausted he was, or how much pressure he was under, he never failed to show up for me. He never really talked about his sister's death, or how he felt about his parents divorcing and practically disappearing from his life afterward. He never really talked about what he himself was going through, and to be honest, I never really asked. At the time, I felt that derailing my future in favor of his was such an incredible sacrifice, that it somehow absolved me from having to give him anything more than that. *Shame on me.*

I gazed out the train window at the changing leaves on the way back to Essex. It was the autumn of our senior year, once again. Well, *his* senior year. I hadn't been alone on the train since the first time, when I visited Kate at Columbia. Then too, I was desperate to make a change. Sometimes, in all honesty, I felt resentful about the plan we made. It wasn't me who lost my funding. But Adam's rationale made perfect sense. It can take years to write a book, and years more to see it published. Adam would have a well-paying position in place before he even graduated. This was the most logical choice to secure our future.

"You look terrible," my mother declared as she watched me step off the train, peering over the top of her oversized designer sunglasses, looking me up and down. Inspecting me. Her blonde bob was shiny and perfectly shaped, not a hair out of place, as if she had slipped on a buttery yellow football helmet before leaving the house. Her pants and blouse were perfectly pressed and hanging neatly upon her slender figure; a matching sweater draped over her shoulders. Matching shoes and jewelry, of course.

"Hello to you too, Mom."

She held her arms open for a hug. Hugs from my mother weren't affection, they were assessments. They were how she made sure I wasn't gaining any weight or wearing any synthetic fabrics.

"You look tired. Are you working too hard? I don't like you working at all, you should be in school." She pushed my long, brown hair away from my face, placed her hands on my cheeks, and turned my head from side to side, examining my eyes in the late afternoon sunlight.

"I'm fine, Mom. You know the plan. As soon as Adam graduates and starts working, I'll finish school."

"As soon as Adam graduates and starts working, he'll promptly leave you behind."

"Mom…"

"Fine. That may not happen. Your father and I like Adam, we really do. But we love you, Elizabeth. You're absolutely brilliant, and we hate seeing your future on hold like this." *I hated it too.*

My parents knew I was working at The Library, I just never told them that it was actually the name of a dive bar just off campus. There was only so much disappointment I could handle from my mother at once. Neither of my parents went to college, which made it all the more important to them that Kate and I did. They had never been afraid to demand excellence from us, or to make their disappointments clearly known.

My mother didn't come from much. She was a beauty queen in her home state of California, and traveled to New York City in her early 20's to become a model. She became a bank teller. It was a win-win for the banks to hire beautiful young women to be their tellers. It attracted the business of professional men with climbing wealth, and the women were often swept off their feet by those men before they could earn raises or promotions. Women at that time – at least the pretty ones – were well-trained to believe their only chance for a good life was to marry well. My father came into the bank one day, and thought she was the most stunning thing he'd ever seen. She thought the same thing about his bank account, which actually belonged to my grandfather of the same name. That's what got him in the door with her, though, and they ended up genuinely falling for each other. My father's family was in the construction business. He poured concrete in the summers during high school, then started full time as a crew leader right after graduation. Eventually, he took over the company when my grandfather retired. My father did pretty well for himself, and once my sister and I came along, they relocated to Connecticut and my mother never had to work again. In her mind, it was horribly backward that I was supporting Adam. She insisted that he would stop finding me and my neuroses the least bit endearing as soon as I no longer benefitted him financially. There was no point in trying to convince her she was wrong.

I learned a lot about architecture from my father growing up. We had a special game we would play whenever we went anywhere. He would point out the unique architectural elements on different houses and buildings, and Kate and I would have to identify them correctly – bonus points if we knew the architectural style. We loved that game, and we often fantasized about how exciting it was going to be when we one day came across the Holy Grail of structures that incorporated one of everything. We imagined how amazing it would feel to walk up to the door and buy it on the spot, no matter the cost. We never considered just building it ourselves. We certainly could have. I guess that felt a little too realistic, and didn't offer the same high as stumbling upon it after an extensive search, desperate to make it our own.

I thought about becoming an architect too, until I took my first creative writing class. I was hooked. While I'd always loved many different creative things, writing was what truly filled my soul. Architecture was what truly filled Kate's soul, and I hoped she would pursue it on a grand scale. She was that good. I didn't want her to go to work for the family construction company, and eventually take over for our father when he retired. I didn't want her to get married, have kids, and give up her career to manage her home and family. That was the path of most of the girls we knew. I knew Kate was meant for something more. I knew I was too.

The interior of my mother's sedan reeked of her strong perfume, combined with the equally strong smell of peppermint candies. She was smoking in her car again, and doing her best to hide it, which always meant she was stressed about something she had no intention of discussing. She had a habit of retreating within herself whenever something was wrong, which was the least flattering characteristic she had, and the only one I seemed to inherit from her. We picked up takeout and headed home to have dinner with my father. I forgot how beautiful Essex was in the fall. The trees had already begun to lose their red-orange leaves, and the toilet paper haphazardly threaded through their branches told me it was homecoming once again, for more than just me.

Driving past the high school gave me a sad feeling now. An expansion had been done to accommodate the influx of students coming over each year from the parochial grade school, now that they had no high school of their own. Everything looked completely different. The inconspicuous door – *my door* – that let you out the back of the school and took you quietly through a clover field, before popping out behind the football stadium, no longer existed. The peaceful clover field was now an overflow parking lot. All evidence of the day Adam Shepherd walked me home from school had been erased, as if it had never really happened. The football stadium received a grand renovation, in honor of the two schools joining together to create one formidable team, and our little public library – *my library* – was torn down to make way for it. Every available surface throughout town had become host to a plaque, banner, or mural urging the football team toward unrelenting victory. Thankfully our old stately home, standing formally just off the corner of Braeburn Street, hadn't changed at all.

I gave my father a hug, taking in the comforting smell of freshly milled lumber that never faded from him. I helped my mother transplant the takeout into serving bowls and set the dining room table. She insisted on a formal and proper presentation, under any and all circumstances. After dinner, my mother said goodnight and went upstairs to get ready for bed. She always headed up around 8:00pm, giving herself plenty of time for a hot bath and her lengthy beauty regimen. If it weren't for this nightly routine, I would have missed out on so many great late-night conversations with my father over the years, usually had while doing the dishes by hand in our quiet, dimly lit kitchen. I always slept so well after those talks. My mother preferred to keep her feelings to herself, and take a pill to help her sleep.

"Can I ask you something?" I picked up the dish towel and prepared myself for the first hand-off.

"Anything," my father replied, handing me a warm, wet plate.

"Was she always like this?"

"Like what?"

"Disapproving, difficult, demanding…"

He smiled at me, somewhat amused. "Your mother is the most insecure woman I've ever met. Beneath that tough exterior is a little girl who grew up being treated like she was never enough. That's why it's so important to her that everything always be so perfect. When someone tells her how beautiful she looks, or how amazing her daughters are, for that moment she allows herself to feel like she's done well."

"If she knows how awful it feels to be treated that way, then how can she do the same thing to me?"

"There's not a day that goes by where your mother doesn't ask me, in one way or another, if she's done enough to ensure you and Kate become strong, successful women. We've been blessed with a good life, and she loves this family very much, but I think part of her wishes she'd done something more with herself. It's the most important thing in the world to her that you and Kate have everything you want in life."

I tapped lightly on the partially opened door to my parents' bedroom, pushing it further open, to find my mother sitting up in bed, reading a book. I had no idea she read. "What are you reading?" I asked softly. She tilted the cover toward me as I entered the room and sat down on the edge of the bed. *Pride and Prejudice.* "I never knew you liked Jane Austen."

"This particular book is the reason you are named Elizabeth Jane," my mother said with a grin, peering over the top of the book at me through her drug store cheaters. "I must have read them all at least a dozen times. This may sound silly to you, Elizabeth, but sometimes I think about the books we'll never have the chance to read, the ones she would have written had she been blessed with a longer life." In that moment, all I could think about was the years of conversations like this one I didn't get to have with my mother.

"That doesn't sound silly to me at all. You know, I read somewhere that she was eleven chapters into her next book when she passed away."

"Really? I wonder what it was about."

"It was called *Sanditon*. It was about a woman who moves to a seaside resort town for a fresh start. The unfinished manuscript was passed around her family for a long time. A few people tried to complete it, I guess, but no one could do it."

"I'm not surprised. I can't imagine a tougher act to follow."

"Me either. It would be impossible to pick up where she left off, without knowing where she intended the story to go, or who the hero was meant to be."

"I'm sure you could do it," she smiled. "You can do anything."

Margaret Fuller

Margaret Fuller was a genius. No, I take that back. Margaret Fuller was a god. Not only had Amy and I read everything she'd ever written, we read everything she'd ever referenced within her writing. In addition to writing critically acclaimed novels, she wrote plays, poetry (for which she won a Nobel prize in 1968), she was an adjunct literature professor, and a renowned literary critic. Her satirical shorter works were often featured in *The New Yorker,* and her novels were published by one of the oldest, most well-known publishing houses in existence, responsible for publishing some of the most important female figures in American literature, like Emily Dickinson and Louisa May Alcott.

She was born in Massachusetts in the 1940s, and according to one of the many articles written about her in *New York Magazine* over the course of her career, she was descended from a Salem woman who was believed to be a witch. Witchcraft was a common theme in her work, and I always wondered if that was due to her ancestry, or if it was simply something her agent conjured up to sell more books. Either way, she was as fascinating as the characters she created and the stories she told.

Margaret was uniquely beautiful, and had once modeled for Andy Warhol. She became part of the New York creative scene in the 1960s, spending time at Warhol's studio, The Factory, which had become the place to be for all of New York's up and coming models, artists, actors, musicians, and writers. On any given night, Margaret could be found partying at The Factory with Warhol and his friends, like David Bowie, Truman Capote, Edie Sedgwick, Keith Haring, and Marilyn Monroe. Even Audrey Hepburn stopped by from time to time. Sometimes I was certain I was born in the wrong era. I often wondered, if my mother had made it as a model in New York City, if she might have been a part of that world. Perhaps she and Margaret would have become best friends, and my life would be better for it.

Margaret learned a great deal about art, music, literature, and film during that time, and used this freshly acquired knowledge to inform her writing. All of her novels were named after her favorite works of art, and included references to her favorite films and songs. Amy and I always made note of these references so we could study the artwork, see the films, and listen to the songs together. Margaret created worlds I wanted to live inside of. Taking the extra step to understand all of her references made her worlds feel all the more real to me.

She never married and always lived alone, with a menagerie of pets that even included wild animals. She was rumored to have had a host of lovers throughout her life, along with some unusual sexual interests. She always wore black, accompanied by one bold accessory – typically a scarf. She owned several rare and classic automobiles, but couldn't be bothered to learn how to drive. She smoked cherry vanilla cigarillos, and drank a lot of heavy-bodied red wine. She rarely stopped working long enough to eat, but when she did, it was always something elaborate. She claimed she didn't care for profanity, despite partaking in it liberally.

Following Adam's graduation, we had a simple wedding at a beautiful orchard in Connecticut, with just our immediate families and a few close friends. I sent an invitation to Amy at her parents' address, but she never responded. I'm not sure if it even got to her. After the ceremony we had a beautiful farm-to-table dinner under the stars. It was casual and sweet. My life seemed to be heading in the right direction again, and something significant, something life-altering, was about to happen. I could feel it coming.

The only job I was able to get in any facet of the New York literary world without a degree was at a small but mighty independent bookstore called The Man Hatter – a play on words referencing The Mad Hatter from *Alice's Adventures in Wonderland* in combination with its Manhattan location. At the time I took the job, I thought it was a clever name. I changed my mind once it became clear that I would have to explain, to at least one person every day, that we did not sell men's hats. The manager was a moron, and I was basically doing his job without the title or the paycheck, but it allowed me the flexibility to return to school, and I could use my downtime to study. Adam was working at Mount Sinai Hospital in Manhattan, and I was finally headed toward graduation with a bachelor's degree in American Literature.

The bookstore was owned by the daughter of a wealthy New York entrepreneur, who had a number of businesses and investment properties throughout the city. It was her pet project. She was able to use her family's high society connections to secure big name authors for readings and signings, as well as get celebrities, socialites, and other prominent people to attend. When the fall event schedule arrived, and I saw Margaret Fuller's name on it, I started preparing immediately. Everything needed to be absolutely perfect for her. I prayed that she would like me, and that she would see something special in me. I fantasized that she would take me to a cocktail party at the home of Professor Susan Smith-Brown, who would recognize me as laundry cart girl and tell everyone how she'd been kicking herself for not taking me under her wing when she had the chance. I fantasized that Amy would see a photograph of me with Margaret Fuller in the *New York Times* and reach out in awe, desperate to rekindle our friendship and hear all about our mutual idol.

I woke up even earlier than Adam the day of the reading. I took extra time with my hair and makeup. I wore a black dress with black high-heeled boots, accompanied by one bold accessory – a red scarf. It was still dark outside when I arrived at the bookstore, and already there were people in line around the corner. I came in through the back of the store. I found a local florist who stocked her favorite black magic roses, imported from Ecuador, and had them delivered the afternoon before. I bought some of the small batch specialty coffee I knew she liked, and set the brewer to start a fresh pot just as she was scheduled to arrive. The line outside became a crowd. The podium and chairs were in place, and everything was perfect. The store phone rang. It was Margaret Fuller's driver, letting me know he was parked in the alleyway. I rushed to the back of the store and opened the door for her, just as the coffee pot kicked on. The day went by in a flash, and I couldn't recall most of the details. The only thing that stood out in my mind was the pair of high school girls who were first in line for the signing, and then hung around all day, just staring at Margaret Fuller with complete admiration. They reminded me so much of Amy and I.

"Excellent work today, young lady," Margaret said to me, as I locked the doors behind the last customer at closing time. "The coffee and flowers were a wonderful touch. You certainly did your homework."

"It was my pleasure, Miss Fuller," I smiled.

"What did you say your name was?"

"Elizabeth."

I was holding my own copy of her new book, still unsigned. She looked up at me over the top of her reading glasses, took it from my hands with a grin, quickly licked the tip of her index finger, and flipped to the title page. "Tell me who you are, Elizabeth," she commanded as she wrote.

"I'm a student at NYU. My husband, Adam, is a doctor at Mount Sinai. I'm in the process of finishing my literature degree, then I plan to get a job in publishing and start writing my first novel. It's such a pleasure to meet you. I admire you so much. I've read everything you've ever written, and everything ever written about you."

"Let me give you a piece of advice, Elizabeth. A woman should never define herself by her marital status, her profession, or her husband's profession." She snapped the book shut with one hand and offered it back to me. "You better come to dinner with me. I need to straighten you out."

✝

The waiter took our coats, we were seated, and Margaret ordered a very old, very expensive, bottle of Cabernet Sauvignon. "Let's try this again, shall we? Tell me who you are, Elizabeth."

"I'm a perpetual student. I love to study and observe. I'm a lover of words, of history, and of architecture. I can't survive a day without coffee. I find the smell of libraries and old books more intoxicating than any flower or perfume. People fascinate me, but I greatly prefer the company of my own thoughts."

"Me too, Elizabeth, me too. Nicely done."

Margaret had the beef bourguignon. I ordered the salade niçoise. We talked for hours, mostly about New York. "The city is spectacular. It's full of excitement, color, and magic. It's a great place to network, to learn, to be inspired...but not a great place to do the real work. I had to get out of the city for that. I moved upstate and never looked back. It was the best decision I ever made."

We finished that bottle of wine, and she ordered another. What a dream come true this was, I thought to myself. A literal prayer answered. I didn't want to miss a single word she said to me. Directly to me. Only to me. At a fancy dinner she invited me to. Margaret Fuller. *I might have been a little drunk.* Just as I thought the evening was coming to an end, she ordered two pieces of flourless dark chocolate cake with an orange whiskey glaze. I ate every bite, though my already full stomach begged me not to. With more alcohol in me than I typically consumed in a year, I told Margaret my entire life story, to that point. I mentioned that Adam had recently been approached about purchasing a small private practice upstate, in a little seaside town called Haven. He really wanted to take the opportunity, but I wasn't sure if that was the life I wanted for myself. It certainly hadn't been part of the plan, but not much had gone to plan anyway.

"Go. Absolutely. I love it upstate. You can't write in the city, Elizabeth. For magazines and newspapers, sure, but not novels. Trust me, I tried. And a job in publishing will swallow you whole. It will run you into the ground and change who you are. The best advice I can give you is to go. Go to Haven, and do nothing but write." Margaret jotted her personal cell phone number and her literary agent's information on the back of her business card, and slid it across the table. She told me to get in touch with her once we were settled in Haven, and that she'd be keeping an eye on my writing progress. "Stop playing it so safe, Elizabeth. When your life is over, all that's left of you will be your story. So you might as well make it an interesting one."

Margaret swallowed the last gulp of her wine. The waiter set down the check and I reached for my purse, knowing there was a fair chance those two bottles of wine alone cost more than I had. "Please," Margaret said, raising both palms off the table. "I've got this. Happy graduation." I hoped she wouldn't notice the sheer relief that had just washed over me.

"Thank you so much, Miss Fuller. This day has been a dream come true."

"Oh honey, we're old friends now. Call me Margaret."

Haven

We stuck everything we'd been saving to buy a house into purchasing the doctor's office in Haven. Dr. Martin Whitmore owned the last remaining private practice on New York's northernmost peninsula, providing care to hundreds of visiting families during the summer months, and to a few dozen locals during the remainder of the year. He was selling his small office building with all of its contents, including the furnishings, medical equipment and supplies, and patient records. It was a modest operation, with a chopper service on contract to get patients to the nearest hospital when necessary. The price was just as modest. When Adam questioned this, Dr. Whitmore simply stated that he cared much more about finding the right person to take over his practice, than in profiting greatly from its sale.

It was still rather unclear as to how this opportunity had fallen into Adam's lap. When Dr. Whitmore called, he said that Adam's name was at the top of a short list of recommendations he'd received from an old colleague at Mount Sinai, but the name of that colleague was never provided. Adam discreetly asked his supervisors at the hospital, but no one seemed to know Dr. Whitmore, or that any private practice had become available for purchase within the state. Being ever the optimist, Adam decided not to look a gift horse in the mouth, and to instead view the unexpected opportunity as a welcomed stroke of good luck.

The purchase process had gone so quickly and easily, it really seemed too good to be true. Most of the negotiations had already taken place remotely over the last several weeks. While Adam and Dr. Whitmore finalized the sale at the doctor's office, I grabbed a cup of coffee and walked the quiet streets of Haven looking for someplace affordable we could live short term while we got to know the area. I spotted a sign reading "apartment for rent" in the window of a metaphysical shop across the street, and went inside. The door jingled as I opened it, and I was immediately hit with the robust, powerful scents of patchouli incense and burning sage. The woman behind the front counter came around the side and shuffled toward the door to greet me, almost losing a flip-flop on the way.

"Hello!" she said, very enthusiastically. She must not get very many customers this late in the season.

"Good morning, I'm here about the apartment for rent?"

"That's what brought you inside, but that's not why you're really here," she laughed with strange delight, as if she was expecting me.

"Do you know why I'm really here?" I asked, curiously.

"You're going to need a friend like me," she smiled. "I'm Sarah." She held out her bony, ring-covered hand. Her long fingernails were painted with a gradient of black to silver glittered polish, and there was an unusual black tattoo peeking out from the bell sleeve of her white peasant top. She reminded me of Carly Simon, with her long, flowing hair and her big, bright smile.

"Elizabeth Farmer," I introduced myself in return.

"Farmer!" she laughed. "You don't need an apartment, Elizabeth Farmer. A farmer needs a farm."

She grabbed my hand and pulled me over to the front counter where her laptop sat. Her long nails and umpteen bracelets clicked and clanged as she quickly pulled up a for sale by owner listing I'd never come across in my own searches. She began to scroll through the photos. It was absolutely beautiful. I'd never seen anything like it before. There was no way could we afford something like this.

"She's been waiting for the right buyer for a very long time. Everybody wants condos and beach houses on the waterfront. Nobody wants to take care of this big, old place in the woods." *I wanted to.* "Six bedrooms. Two bathrooms. A big kitchen with a butler's pantry. Look at all those built-ins! It's perfect for you! I know the family, and the place has been very well taken care of. You could probably get a really great deal on it." How could she possibly know what's perfect for me, I thought. She didn't know the first thing about me. That said, she was absolutely right. If the Holy Grail of houses was hiding here in Haven, it was my duty to make every effort to purchase it on the spot.

"It's beautiful. I've been watching the real estate listings for the past few weeks. I wonder how I missed this place." I told her that my husband was purchasing the doctor's office today. She didn't seem surprised.

"She didn't want to be stumbled upon, Elizabeth Farmer. She wanted to be presented to you. She's meant to be yours, you know."

I held up my phone to take a picture of her laptop screen, but Sarah quickly closed it and insisted she personally call the owner on my behalf for an immediate showing. I agreed. Not because I believed in what Sarah said, but because I absolutely loved the house. Because owning was always better than renting. Because a big, beautiful home like this was much more appropriate for a self-employed physician and a best-selling author than a small apartment above a metaphysical shop. We'd already paid our dues. It was time to go big or go home. To stop playing it so safe. Maybe we could negotiate a no money down or lease to own option, if the owner was that desperate to sell. I texted Adam to meet me at the metaphysical shop as soon as he was finished, so we could go take a look at it.

Sarah picked up a deck of tarot cards. "Let your higher self choose the right card for you," Sarah said softly as she closed her eyes and began to shuffle. She opened one eye and peeked down as a card fell from the deck. "Never mind, that's your card right there," she laughed, picking up the card and flipping it over on the counter. The Sun. She grabbed the well-worn guidebook from beside her on the counter and read: "The Sun is shining on you! It's finally your time for success and happiness. You feel confident and full of hope. This is a time to rejoice, a time for pleasure and good fortune. A time for life to begin anew, and all your dreams to finally come true." *Yes, please.*

The bell hanging above the shop door jingled as Adam entered the store. The sun had finally come out from behind the clouds and streamed in behind him. The Sun. My fortune was already coming true. Adam smiled as he walked toward us. The deal was done.

"*That's* your husband?"

"Sarah, this is my husband, Adam. Adam, this is Sarah." Adam smiled and said hello.

"He's adorable! Oh my God, you are so blessed! Here, take this," she dug around in a bowl on the counter, selecting a quarter-sized green polished stone and pressing it into my hand, "Aventurine is for opportunity and luck. Go see your farm, Elizabeth Farmer!" she laughed.

We hopped in the Jeep and started the short drive along the shoreline, to just outside of town. We could get a peek at the water through the trees. It was the same beautiful blue-gray color as Adam's eyes. I proceeded to tell him everything I knew about the house. I tried to pull up the property listing Sarah had shown me on my phone, but it didn't seem to exist anywhere. All I had was the lot marker code and a few ambiguous directions from Sarah that included "you'll just know." She was right about one thing for certain, this property definitely did not want to be stumbled upon by just anyone.

"We can take a look, but I wouldn't get your hopes up," Adam said. "I don't know if we can even qualify for a home loan, we just put almost everything we have into buying the doctor's office."

We drove slowly down Haven Hill Road, past Hillside Cemetery, watching the lot markers for the right code. We pulled onto the long, winding blacktop driveway marked with the lot code HHS-1111. A short offshoot of the driveway led to another residence – a smaller, cottage-style house that looked similar to the large house Sarah had shown me. It must have been part of the original property at one time, maybe a carriage house, since it was so near to the main road.

"Oh, that's not bad," Adam commented. "Not too much to take care of. We could make that work."

"That's not the same place she showed me. It must be further ahead."

We continued up the driveway, which was really a road unto itself, lined with the most beautiful white-blossomed trees. It was unusual to see such fresh blossoms on the trees this late in the season. I knew what Adam had to be thinking. He was probably wondering how we were going to cut all this grass in the summer, and rake all these leaves in the fall, and plow all this snow in the winter, and tend all these gardens in the spring. This place was institutional in size, and no doubt required a number of routine caregivers. Just then, the trees parted ways like a dramatic theater curtain, revealing a glorious white gothic farmhouse at the top of the hill.

There it was.

The Holy Grail of houses, with one of everything. It was meticulously maintained, and the ornate detailing was exquisite. It was a goddess of wood and stone. A place to be worshipped. We got out of the Jeep and stood there for a moment, gazing upward at the massive white structure. I was instantly captured by it. The moment my feet touched the ground, it had a hold on me. I could feel it through the soles of my shoes. Sarah was absolutely right; it was meant to be mine.

The house stood center stage, with a few matching outbuildings clustered nearby. Each structure was surrounded by beautiful gardens, with flagstone paths connecting them. There was a pasture on two sides of the property, which nature had painted with wildflowers and tall grasses, and the other two sides met with the dense neighboring woods.

An older woman suddenly appeared in the screen door of the wrap-around porch, startling us both. "C'mon in," she said, holding the door open long enough for Adam to catch it and usher me through. "Coffee's on."

"I'm Elizabeth Farmer," I declared as we entered the large eat-in kitchen from the wrap-around porch, "This is my husband, Adam Shepherd. Your home is just stunning."

"Well, thank you. Pleased to meet you both. I'm Mary Wade." She poured three cups of coffee. "Are you folks tourists?" She watched me with pride as I brought the cup of coffee to my face with both hands and breathed it in, my eyes closing as I enjoyed the rich, strong aroma.

"We're relocating to Haven," Adam replied. "I'll be taking over Dr. Whitmore's medical practice."

"Oh good, it's about time Marty hung it up. The ladies will sure love you," she said, looking Adam up and down. Dr. Whitmore had apparently made a similar comment. Mary pried the cover from a tin of homemade chocolate chip cookies and placed it next to the coffee cups.

"Help yourselves. They're fresh. And what do you do, young lady?" she asked, turning to me.

"I'm an author," I replied. It felt really good to say those words, even though they didn't quite feel true.

"You don't say…We had a writer in the family once. A long time ago. Mostly just farmers, though. My daughter paints real well. I don't have a creative bone in my body, it skipped right over me." Mary began to look around the room, pointing with her cup of coffee in her hand. "The house was built in the mid-1800s. Original hardwood floors throughout. Vaulted ceilings. Original cabinetry. All of it made by hand. Lots of built-ins. Wainscoting. Crown molding."

My father always said historic homes were infinitely better than new builds, even though he made his living building new houses. They had character, and were built to stand the test of time. Back then, when people built a homestead, they did so with intention. They chose the perfect location, with the perfect views, and perfectly positioned it to harness everything nature had to share. Not like today, where the average home is built on a small lot, sandwiched in between two other small lots, close enough to see what your neighbors have on their dinner plates. A sea of plain grass laid out behind it, barely a tree left standing, and a slab of cold concrete outside the standard issue patio door.

"There's a butler's pantry off the kitchen here, with a pass-through to the dining room." We followed Mary from the kitchen through the galley-style butler's pantry, lined with countertops and cabinets, into the formal dining room. The woodwork was unbelievably pristine, as if it were brand new. "The dining room empties out into the living room, the study is just through there, and there's one bedroom and bath here on the first floor, for guests. I've been using those myself the last year or so. I can't manage the stairs like I used to."

Under Mary's watchful eye, we walked the perimeter of each room on the first floor. Everything was so neat, clean, and bright. Not so much as a small stain or stray thread to be found. I found it hard to believe that Mary could be managing this all on her own.

"My daughter lives in Florida now. She just got divorced, so as soon as I'm rid of this place, I'll be heading down there to live with her and help with my grandbabies. There's nothing left for me up here anymore, it's just me and the ghosts."

"Ghosts?" I asked.

Mary chuckled at my unease. "Well, I'm sure you folks noticed on your way through, Haven becomes a bit of a ghost town once all the vacationers head out." That was a quick save on Mary's part, but I was certain it wasn't really what she meant.

"Florida will be nice," I shouted from the study, swiftly changing the topic while admiring the hand-crafted bookcases. They were full of interesting old books that looked to be arranged very specifically, though I could not make sense of their order. What a lovely writing room this would be, overlooking the beautiful flower gardens. I could already imagine my first novel coming to life here.

"If I can ever get out of here," she continued. "I've been waiting for the right buyer for a few years now. Most folks are looking for something low maintenance, and in town. Something they can easily leave behind when the weather gets too rough. This place is a full-time job and then some, not to mention isolated. Say, head on upstairs without me. I have to sit down."

We started up the open staircase to the second floor, where there were five more bedrooms and another bathroom. While that was great plenty, it seemed as though there ought to be more to it, given the overall size of the house. Each room was tastefully and minimally furnished with simple, classic pieces and calming neutral tones. Everything was unusually timeless, and perfectly placed. There was nothing to distract from all the amazing architectural details. From this high on the hill, there were even water views from some of the rooms on the second floor. Strangely, there were no personal belongings at all. No photographs on the walls or tables, no clothes in the closets…not even in the bedroom and bathroom Mary claimed to be using for the last year. I hope there's a good thrift store in town, I thought to myself, if I was to have any prayer of furnishing a place of this size.

"Everything stays with the house," Mary shouted upward from the bottom of the staircase, as if she could hear my thoughts. "It's all handmade. Sturdy. Built from the trees right here on the property. So is the house, for that matter. Not like those cookie cutter condos they keep slapping up along the waterfront."

I looked at Adam and smirked, because I knew that's exactly what he'd prefer we were looking at. He was hoping for something much smaller and newer, close enough to walk or bike to the doctor's office, that wouldn't require a great deal of upkeep. The on-call nature of his profession meant never knowing if you'd be able to keep your personal commitments. The house and grounds were certainly immense, but somehow Mary was managing it on her own, so I saw no reason I couldn't.

We took a quick peek at the third floor from the top of the stairs. It was a wide open and empty space, unused, but still as well kept as the rest of the house. Not a speck of dust or a trace of infestation. The entire house was unbelievably immaculate. We took the back staircase down to the kitchen, where Mary was sitting at the table waiting for us, finishing her coffee. Adam didn't even ask if I wanted to make an offer, he knew I was in love the minute we walked through the door. There was just something so alluring about it. I could practically hear it whispering my name.

"We're definitely interested. I'll need to give our bank a call this week, and try to get an inspector up here…" Adam started, but Mary cut him off.

"Look, I like you folks. I can see you love the house, and I have a feeling you'll take excellent care of the old girl. There's nothing wrong with her, she just needs more attention than I've got left to give. There's no mortgage on this place, there never has been. The taxes are low. The utilities are next to nothing, if you're mindful. The fireplaces are all you need in the winter months, and there's enough wood cut and stacked out in the barn to last you for the next few years. I've got the deed right here in the kitchen drawer. If you can come back in a week with fifty thousand in cash, the house is all yours."

"But the listing Sarah showed me was for…"

"I know what the listing says. Do you want the house or not?" Adam looked rightfully skeptical.

"Yes!" I blurted out. "We want it."

The Farm

Over the next week, we sold most of what we owned and withdrew every penny that was left in our bank account. Adam didn't have much in his 401K this early into his career, but after the penalties for early withdrawal, it was just enough to make up the difference. We headed back to Haven in Adam's Jeep, packed with what little we still owned. On my lap was my cherished jade plant, and a manila envelope containing fifty thousand dollars in cash. We drove in nervous silence, while I played out every possible scenario in my mind. What if Mary had already left, after selling the property to someone else? What if we arrived to find Mary dead at the bottom of the stairs, and if so, do we take the house? What if Mary was actually senile, or insane, and didn't remember the strange deal she had made with us? What if Mary had been killing prospective buyers for years, burying them on the property, and pocketing fifty grand per couple? (That could make a really good book.) Perhaps Sarah got a cut for sending new people her way. Or, worst case scenario, what if Mary came to her senses and decided she wanted the full listing price? We might end up living in that small apartment above the metaphysical shop after all.

We heard Mary moving around inside, talking to herself, as Adam tapped on the kitchen screen door. "C'mon in," she hollered. "I'm glad you came back."

Adam set a short and simple contract for deed on the counter, as his attorney friend from the hospital advised. Mary had the deed sitting out as well, tucked under the corner of a Keurig box.

"A housewarming gift," she winked at me. She quickly scratched her signature onto the contract for deed without reading it, slid the deed out from under the box corner, and slapped it down on top of the contract. It was already signed.

The deal was done.

"Do you think you'll miss it here?"

"I'm ready for some peace and quiet," she answered.

"Really? I can't imagine a quieter, more peaceful place than this."

Mary stared at me for a good, long time. "I'm exhausted, Miss Farmer. There are 150 years' worth of my family still hanging around here. Keeping a close eye on things. You'll see. They'll be nagging after you to keep the place up. If you take good care of things, if you're respectful, then everything will be just fine. If not…well then, good luck to you."

It didn't take long to unpack, since the house was already fully furnished and we owned little more than our clothes. We had nothing we didn't need, and everything had a place. Every large, bright space was perfectly appointed, but completely impersonal. Almost clinical in its perfection. Perhaps it was the fast and strange way in which we had purchased the property, or the fact that there was very little of us represented here, but it didn't feel like ours at all. I wondered if it ever would. A week ago, it was calling to me. It was practically pulling me inside. Now there was just silent nothingness.

Adam was at the doctor's office from sunrise to sunset every weekday, and he would be on call every night and weekend until he was able to hire some help. Dr. Whitmore mentioned it might be tough to get anyone remotely qualified to come this far north. The practice came with an already full schedule of local patients, and he had to bring himself up to speed on every one of them. He was home long enough to have a bite to eat and head up to bed shortly afterward. He absolutely loved it, and I was so happy for him, but I was already getting lonely. I had mistakenly assumed that being isolated together would bring us closer.

I spent my first few weeks in Haven doing everything but writing, and I was getting more and more frustrated with each passing day. Adam's alarm went off every morning at 5:00am. I would make a pot of coffee and pack him a healthy lunch while he showered and dressed. Once he was out the door, I would pour myself a cup of coffee, sit down at the desk in the study, and stare at a blank Word document. Sometimes I would daydream for an hour or two while staring out the windows, and tell myself I was concepting. Sometimes I would spend an hour or two typing whatever came into my mind, read it over in disgust, and then delete it. I didn't allow myself to select all and hit the delete key. As a personal punishment for the absolute garbage I had just written, I forced myself to push the backspace key over and over, and watch every letter, every word, that should have never been typed into existence, disappear one by one until the document was blank again. Then I typically spent the rest of the day washing things that were already clean, and straightening things that were already tidy. I would rearrange things, only to put them right back where they started. I was surprised there weren't tiny pencil marks near everything, God forbid anything should be nudged an inch from its perfect placement. I was a little jealous of all these inanimate things, so well cared for, knowing without question exactly where they belonged, and how valuable they were.

I thought about cutting fresh flowers from the beautiful gardens, and placing them in vases around the house to cheer myself up and make things feel homier, but Mary's odd warning rang in my ears constantly. I couldn't be certain if cutting the flowers would qualify as being disrespectful. I wished I had thought to ask for her number in Florida, so I could call for clarification, but I got the sense she wasn't interested in hearing from us once the deal was done. Adam insisted it was just something she said to make sure we took good care of her family's homestead. We were the first people outside Mary's family ever to own it. There was no doubt some guilt attached to being the person responsible for the property leaving her family's hands. I felt foolish for putting any stock whatsoever in her strange and threatening final words, but there was something about this place that was unsettling enough to make me believe them. It felt both dead and alive at the same time. It felt bustling with activity, while remaining empty, quiet, and still. It felt off balance and distorted, despite being impeccably straight and level for its age. It felt like the house was pleased with itself for enticing me so easily, and now it would delight in showing me what a poor, impulsive decision I'd made.

From an architectural standpoint, it was a magnificent marvel, light years ahead of its time. It was constructed using unpretentious natural materials taken directly from the landscape, but was designed in such an exceptional way, it was anything but modest. I couldn't wait for Kate and my father to see it, to study it. Corridors got darker and narrower just before you entered expansive, light-filled spaces, creating a feeling of compression and release that left you physically disoriented. Doors led to other doors, which led to angular, awkward spaces, and sharp turns resulted in abrupt stopping points. I had no recollection of seeing any of those strange features when we first toured the house, but they obviously must have been there. It was as if every square foot of this house was designed to challenge what you thought you knew. Every day I noticed at least one thing that I couldn't be certain had been there the day before.

I took my bold red scarf, the one I had worn the day I met Margaret Fuller, and closed it inside one of the upstairs windows. This window was at the end of a hallway that all things suggested should continue on, yet I was standing at the end of it. I went downstairs, out the front door, and walked around the entire exterior of the house. The scarf was not visible in any window. When I went back inside and returned to the window at the end of the hallway, the scarf was still there, exactly as I had placed it. While this was certainly confusing, the strangest of my daily observations was that the house was oddly synchronous. Something always stopped just as another thing started. Something always turned on just as something else turned off. Something seemingly ordinary always occurred at the exact moment I set foot into any room, or just as I stepped out of it. The house had a personality. A rhythm. A pulse.

There were days I would just walk around the house and grounds looking at everything, taking in every careful detail, thinking it was the most enchanting and beautiful place I had ever been, feeling like I absolutely belonged there and I never wanted to leave. It was intoxicating. Euphoric even. Surely there were few authors with the good fortune to write in such an inspiring, magical place.

There were also days I felt so paranoid and anxious, that I couldn't seem to get out of the house fast enough. I felt like I was being observed, followed, and perhaps even taunted. I peeked out the corner of the shower curtain, fully expecting someone to be standing in the doorway, staring at me. I felt ushered out of rooms, and hurried up or down the stairs. I stood in front of closet doors, afraid to open them and find someone inside. I felt someone looking over my shoulder and breathing down my neck whenever I was in the kitchen. I had spontaneous hot flashes, immediately followed by chills. My body shook and my pulse raced. I routinely experienced nausea, headaches, and blurred vision. I often burst into laughter or tears, and for no apparent reason.

I decided to tell Adam what I'd been experiencing, and his response was exactly what I expected it to be. "It's an old house, Elizabeth, built by hand. You understand the quirks that come along with that. Everything is new and strange right now. Remember when we first moved into the walk-up?"

We were so excited to be moving into our first apartment together, that we failed to notice the serious lack of outlets. And lights. And heating vents. Not to mention, every time the refrigerator ran, it sounded like a helicopter gearing up to take flight. At first those things were annoying, but over time they became comical and endearing. A few power strips, a few lamps, a space heater…and we placed a magnet over the sweet spot on the side of the refrigerator where it could be kicked into submission. It was our first place all to ourselves, and we made it work.

"It took us months to get used to everything there, and we've only been here for a few weeks. Give it some time. If you're not comfortable working alone out here during the day, come into town with me and write at the doctor's office or the coffee house until you're feeling more settled." As far as my physical ailments, he explained that it would also take time for our bodies to adjust to the different elevation and climate, that our proximity to the water and the woods meant a new host of allergens, on top of the seasonal change.

He was right. He was always right. Though it thoroughly annoyed me when he spoke to me like a doctor speaking to his patient, I was grateful that at least one of us had a firm grip on reality. *What was wrong with me?* We were blessed to live in such a beautiful place, in an incredible home that was ours free and clear. Nobody else our age could say that. Adam owned an established private practice that doctors twenty years his senior were still working toward obtaining. We were the beneficiaries of unbelievably good fortune, and for some reason, I was determined to create an issue where there wasn't one. I was desperate for any possible cause, outside of my own self, to explain why I was incapable of writing anything worth saving. The house was taunting you? Are you kidding me? *Come on, Elizabeth. Pull yourself together.*

Sarah

I threw on my favorite sweater, grabbed my book bag, and rode into town with Adam. Fall was really setting in now, and there was a thick fog accompanying the temperature shift. The weather on the peninsula was very unpredictable, I was learning. Still being in Haven after tourist season was over felt wrong somehow, like still being in a store after it had closed for the night. Mary Wade was right, it was a little bit like a ghost town, quiet and still, with an eerie whistle to the wind that glided inland over the water's surface.

I started the short walk from the doctor's office to the coffee house, and found myself standing outside the metaphysical shop. Sarah was inside. I knocked on the glass of the storefront window and waved to her, assuming that the store would be closed for the season. She came shuffling toward the door in her bedroom slippers, wrapping her long cardigan sweater more tightly around her, and motioning for me to come inside. The bell jingled as she pushed the door open and held it there, ushering me in.

"Elizabeth Farmer!" she hollered, followed by her distinctive laugh. "Get in here! Can you believe how fast the weather turned? How's the writing going?" I didn't recall telling her that I was a writer. Maybe Sarah really did…know things.

"Hi Sarah," I smiled. "I wanted to return your stone and say thank you. We loved the house you recommended, and we bought it."

"I know! You keep it. It was a gift," she laughed. "Your adventure is just beginning!"

I thanked her again. I began to look around the store, with Sarah right behind me like an excited puppy, explaining what everything was and what it could be used for. "I just needed to get out of the house today," I confessed, looking over my shoulder in her direction.

"That's what brought you inside, but that's not why you're really here," she declared, just as she had before.

"Do you know why I'm really here?" I stopped moving and looked her in the eyes, praying she had an answer to that question, because I didn't.

"I told you, Elizabeth Farmer, you're going to need a friend like me." Fair enough.

I grabbed two pumpkin spice lattes and two carrot cake muffins from the coffee house down the street and returned to the metaphysical shop, handing one of each to Sarah. We sat down together by the storefront window for a while, warming up next to the old iron radiator, watching a bumbling old couple try to switch out the streetlamp banners from summer to fall, through the mist and fog.

"Tell me about yourself, Sarah." She seemed delighted to be asked.

"Well, I always say, I'm a gypsy soul, like my mother was. She moved to Haven to be with my father, but she was never really happy here. I left Haven the day after my high school graduation. I couldn't wait to get out of here! I was certain nothing exciting was ever going to happen to me if I stayed. I took a greyhound bus all the way to California, and joined a spiritual collective. I'm a natural healer, you know. There I learned about massage, reiki, meditation, acupuncture, divination…whatever they would teach me. Everything was done on equal work share. If I helped prepare a meal or retrieve water from the natural spring, I was given a portion. For every hour I spent working on the property, I received one lesson. It was wonderful, for a while. Well, long story short, they figured out I have real abilities around the same time I figured out they were all full of shit," she laughed.

I was beginning to see that Sarah laughed at everything. When something was really funny, when something really wasn't funny at all, and just about every occasion in between.

"They locked me in a room beneath the sanctuary and forced me to speak to the spirits for them. Once you unlock the door to the spirit world, Elizabeth Farmer, you can't control who comes through it. I was trapped down there for months, with all manner of things, until someone finally took pity on me and helped me escape. She gave me a change of clothes, a bottle of fresh water, and the little bit of money she had.

I got as far as I could by bus and hitchhiked from there, until I wound up in New Orleans. I lived on the streets in the French Quarter for a while, doing tarot readings for tourists so I'd have money to eat. One day, I did a reading for this really cute guy, and he invited me to work out of his tattoo shop. I ended up marrying him. We were really happy for a couple of months, until I caught him cheating on me.

I got an annulment and planned to get on a bus and come home, but then I met a guy at the bus depot who was touring with his band. They invited me to travel with them for the last stretch of their tour, selling t-shirts at their concerts in exchange for the ride. I got to see a lot of the country! Jacksonville, Atlanta, Charlotte, Philadelphia, Boston... That's when the spirits told me I needed to get home to my mom, but by the time I got here, she was gone." Sarah looked around the room. "This was her shop. I took it over after she died. So here I am, right back where I started, the one place I swore I'd never end up." Tears began to well up in her big, brown eyes. She lifted her hand to wipe them before they could smudge her makeup. "It's kind of you to talk to me like this. I don't have anyone to talk to." I think Sarah needed a friend like me, too.

We talked for the rest of the morning. Sarah had multiple fascinating layers. I envied all of the adventures she'd had, from the fantastic, to the frightening, to the funny. She was a great storyteller. Maybe she should be the one writing books. At the very least, she'd make a great character, if I ever managed to write something.

"Did you know Dr. Whitmore well?"

"Oh, yes. He's a wonderful man. He and my mom were good friends my whole life. This was his building. He lived in the other upstairs apartment. The one you thought you came here to rent," she laughed. "By the time she realized something wasn't right and told him about it, it was too late. All he could do was take care of her until she passed. Dr. Whitmore had always been in love with her, and she grew to love him too. I think that's really why he started looking for a buyer. He couldn't bear to look at her apartment door every day, after she was gone. He couldn't bear to look out his office window at her empty shop."

I told Sarah that when I saw Adam for the first time, I was instantly drawn to him. I knew on some level that we were supposed to be together. She told me that probably meant we were soul mates. I told her everything we'd overcome and sacrificed to get to this point in time, and that while moving to Haven was technically for Adam, I had high hopes it would be a good move for me, too. I shared with her my lifelong dream of becoming an author. I told her I'd been developing story fragments in my mind for years, jotting down notes on random surfaces, making sketches, and taking photos. The ground work was all there. I felt so beyond ready to sit down and start writing, especially now that I was in the perfect place to do so. I even had a famous, best-selling author as my personal friend and mentor. I had her agent ready to work with me as soon as I had something worthwhile to send her. But the story refused to come out of my mind and into the real world. It was locked within me, and I didn't know why. Whenever I sat down to type, all that spilled onto the page was repetitive nonsense.

"I don't suppose you have a cure for writer's block somewhere in here?"

Sarah laughed and shook her head, no. "Writer's block doesn't really exist. Maybe it's just not time to write, Elizabeth Farmer. Maybe it's time to learn." She pointed out the front window, across the street, to the Haven Public Library.

I'd always loved libraries. To me, they were a glorious place of worship. As soon as I walked up the wide stone steps and through the heavy double doors, I felt a wave of familiar comfort wash over me. My boots echoed in the quiet, open space as I walked toward the information desk and asked for directions to the local history archives. I took my time getting there, taking in the careful design of the building and the treasures it held, from paintings and pottery by local artisans, to sculptural pieces of driftwood and rusted ship wreckage that had washed ashore over the years. I could feel the energy emanating from them. They all had stories trapped inside of them, too.

The Haven Historical Society was housed within the Haven Public Library. On the walls outside its offices on the second floor were dozens of framed maps and photographs that showed how the area and the town had changed over time, leading me down the hallway toward the local history section. I set my sweater and book bag down on a small table by the window, and began scanning the heavy wooden shelves. Oh, how I loved books. Audio books and eBooks were ideal in certain circumstances, but there would never be a replacement, in my mind, for real, tangible books. The weight, the texture, the materials, the scent… I ran my fingers along their spines as I slowly made my way up and down the rows, examining them all closely. I carefully selected a small stack of local history books and returned to my table to dive into them. I had the whole floor to myself.

It wasn't until the sconces lining the walls dimmed that I realized it was dark outside and the library was closing. As I grabbed my things and hurried toward the staircase, I noticed a small round table near the top of the stairs displaying copies of a self-published book titled *The Legacies and Legends of Haven*. Somehow, I got the feeling this book was why Sarah sent me here. I slipped a copy into my bag, not having time to buy it before closing. It was a library, after all. I didn't see the harm. I reached the bottom of the stairs just as the librarian was pulling down the key from its hook to lock the heavy front doors. She jumped when she heard the sound of my footsteps coming up behind her, and turned around slowly with one hand over her chest. "Young lady, that's right," she seemed relieved. "I'd forgotten anyone else was here."

I was instantly reminded of the time Amy and I hid in the bathroom at the Essex County Library because we thought it would be really fun to spend the night in the library by ourselves. Apparently, unlike Haven, the curators of the Essex County Library did a walk through before they locked up for the night. I'd since outgrown the idea that voluntary captivity might be a reasonably good time.

After dinner, Adam headed upstairs to shower and get some sleep. I sat down in the antique banker's chair behind the gorgeous mahogany desk in the study and pulled everything from my book bag, startled by the author's photo on the back of the book I'd taken. As a little girl, one of my favorite books was *The Giving Tree* by Shel Silverstein, but the author's headshot on the back of the jacket cover scared the hell out of me. I Scotch taped a piece of typing paper over it so I wouldn't have to look at him anymore, and I wondered how someone so terrifying could write something so lovely. This author gave Shel Silverstein a run for his money. I really wanted to cover the photo, but I didn't want to risk damaging a book that didn't yet belong to me.

The Legacies and Legends of Haven was written by Dr. Stephen Lawrence, a literature professor at Kingston University in nearby North Haven, and a past president of the Haven Historical Society. The photo showed Dr. Lawrence sitting at his desk in his office at the university, surrounded by artifacts, stacks of books, and piles of papers. He looked exactly as you'd expect an old literature professor to look, right down to the elbow patches on his tweed jacket – on the right. On the left, however, he was bald with purplish red, rippled skin. He appeared to have been badly burned, but impossibly, in a clean line exactly down the middle of him. His left ear was completely melted shut and his partially-open left eye was a cloudy white. His reddish-brown hair and beard stopped precisely in the center of him, as if half of a man and half of a demon had somehow been fused together. The classic New England seascape on the cover of the book was a welcomed bore. The book was dedicated to the love of his life, Melinda. I scanned the table of contents, skimmed the introduction, and began reading chapter one.

The northernmost peninsula of New York had always been one of the most beautiful landscapes in the country. But the harsh, rocky terrain and unpredictable weather made it impossible to grow crops or raise livestock in the area, which is why Native American tribes had never really settled in this part of the state. While the peninsula saw its share of European explorers as early as the 1600s, its first permanent settlers didn't arrive until the early 1800s. For close to 200 years, while the rest of New York (and the United States as a whole) was being populated and developed, New York's northernmost peninsula stood still in time, dormant and overlooked. The only way in or out was by boat, at the time. Its eventual settlers made their living largely through the harvesting of timber and fish. By the mid-1800s, the over-harvesting of those resources, combined with the establishment of new land transportation options, led to a rise in tourism that became the most reliable income source for the area.

There was only one farm on the entire peninsula, established by the Rowe family, who arrived by ship from origins unknown. The land they chose to purchase and settle on was no more fertile than any other, but the farm they established – to everyone's amazement – inexplicably flourished. The rising costs of transporting food into the area had everyone turning to the Rowe farm as their primary source of sustenance. By 1870, the Rowes had become one of the wealthiest, most beloved families in the entire area. They began a number of other thriving businesses, including a public market and an apothecary, and funded the establishment of many key institutions, such as the library, the school, and the area's first bank.

In that moment it occurred to me, this strange and beautiful place that everybody loved, yet nobody wanted, this place that now belonged to us, had to be the Rowe farm. No wonder Mary Wade had made such a strange and intimidating insistence regarding its upkeep. This property was a historical landmark and a cherished local treasure, well beyond its architectural significance. According to Dr. Lawrence's book, some people believed it was built upon a nexus – a natural source of energy, which is how it derived its ability to grow crops in barren ground, and well past the normal growing season. Some believed the Rowe family brought mysterious powers here with them, which led to their unfathomable success. I stayed awake all night finishing Dr. Lawrence's book. It outlined each of Haven's founding families, recounted every local shipwreck, and chronicled every significant landmark, milestone and mysterious occurrence from the town's formation to the time of the book's publication. The story that pulled me in the most was that of Eliza Jane Rowe. We had almost the same name, she looked a little bit like me, and she was also an aspiring author. She must be the writer in the family that Mary Wade had mentioned. Dr. Lawrence's book noted that Eliza Rowe was a brilliant and strange young woman, ahead of her time in many ways. She lived here with her parents, suffering from severe anxiety and unexplained physical ailments, until the time of her death at a fairly young age. She never married or had children. It was believed that she locked herself away after the death of her beloved brother, Ethan, shutting out the world and doing nothing but writing until her untimely passing. How awful for her, I thought. She must have been very close to her brother, like Adam was to his sister. I couldn't even imagine how much it would have damaged me if I'd lost Kate when we were growing up – or my best friend, Amy, who had once been like a sister to me.

Eliza passed away before she could complete her first novel, never realizing her dream of becoming a published author. What's more, her unfinished manuscript was never located following her death. Some of the greatest works of American literature were written in the late 1800s. I bet Eliza read them all, as I had. I wondered if her manuscript was any good, and if it would've had the potential to become a piece of classic American literature, if she'd been able to complete it. Maybe it was still in the house somewhere, I thought. I should take a look around for it. I'd love to read it.

"Are you feeling better?" Adam asked on the drive into town the next morning.

"I feel fine," I replied, rather confused. He must have thought I hadn't come to bed the previous night because I wasn't feeling well.

"I'm glad. Did you have a nightmare? You were really cold, and clinging to me. I asked if you were okay, but you didn't answer me." I hadn't been to bed at all. I assumed he must have had a dream.

I made a pot of coffee and helped with administrative work at the doctor's office until the library opened. There was a backlog of patient files to be updated and put away, going back six months before Adam took over. Among those patients was Mary Wade.

"Hey Adam, take a look at this," He rolled himself over to me in his office chair and leaned in. "Mary Wade has kidney disease, she's in renal failure. And it says here she has no next of kin. Wasn't she going to live with her daughter in Florida?"

"Hm. That's definitely what she told us. I'll see what I can find out."

I registered for a library card, bought Dr. Lawrence's book and promptly covered up his photo, then went straight back to the local history shelves. I spent the entire day studying every birth, death, and marriage record on file, dating back to the town's formation. I read every obituary, studied every photograph, and read every news article. I was determined to get to the bottom of everything that was unexplained about the area, the land, and the Rowe farm. There was so much information that was either missing, redacted, or incomplete.

It was time I met Dr. Lawrence.

Dr. Lawrence

First, I called Dr. Lawrence. The receptionist for the English Department at Kingston University informed me that he was giving a lecture, and transferred me to his office voicemail. My message simply stated that my name was Elizabeth Farmer, that I was new to the area, and that I would like to meet with him to discuss his book. He did not return my call.

Next, I sent Dr. Lawrence an email, through the faculty directory on the university website. I referenced my earlier voicemail message, and added that I was an aspiring author studying Haven's history. He did not reply.

Finally, I drove to Kingston University. I threw my book bag over my shoulder and walked the campus, hoping to run into him. Part of me was eager to find him quickly and get the answers I was looking for, and part of me was simply enjoying spending time on a college campus again. I'd always hoped to get my master's degree one day, so I could become an adjunct literature instructor and further follow in the footsteps of Margaret Fuller.

Kingston University was an incredible place. Every historic Federal-style structure was constructed of centuries old red brick, reminiscent of the post-revolutionary architecture I'd revered throughout my time in New York City. I could feel the past all around me. This campus had intrigue. It had secrets. It had ghosts. The lawns and landscaping were lush and perfectly manicured, and there wasn't a speck of loose trash on the ground. It was quieter and more orderly than a college campus had any right to be. I found my way to the English department offices and hung around, waiting, as long as it took for Dr. Lawrence to return. He finally arrived in the early afternoon, and exchanged greetings with the receptionist as he hurried down the hallway toward his office. "Dr. Lawrence?" I followed him through his office door.

"Yes?" he didn't stop until he reached his desk, picking up a small pile of papers from the corner and turning toward me. The left side of him was even more startling in person. I hoped the moment it took for me to gather myself and speak didn't feel as uncomfortably long and awkward to him as it did to me.

"My name is Elizabeth Farmer. I've been trying to reach you."

"Oh, yes. Miss Farmer. You are persistent, aren't you?" He thumbed through the pile of papers as he spoke, without bothering to look up at me. "I'm afraid I already have a teaching assistant for this term, but thank you for your interest."

"That's not why I'm here, Professor. I'm not looking for a job."

"Oh, I see. Then what can do for you? I have a lecture to get to."

Dr. Lawrence gathered his things, breezed past me, and stood next to the door with his hand on the knob, impatiently waiting to see me out.

"My husband and I recently purchased the Rowe farm in Haven. I've been spending time at the Haven Public Library researching the history of the area and the property, which led me to your book. I was wondering, is there anything else you found in your research, anything that wasn't in your book? Are there any additional resources you might be able to recommend?"

Dr. Lawrence looked out his office door and then back at me, shut the door, and came back to his desk. He picked up the phone and dialed the receptionist, asking her to reach his teaching assistant and have her give his last lecture of the day. He cleared a stack of books and papers off of the wooden chair across from his desk, motioning for me to sit down, as he slowly lowered himself into his desk chair.

"That's not possible, Miss Farmer. That property has never been bought or sold."

I told him I'd been shown the property listing, which had never come up in my own searches for housing in the area, and then the listing seemed to just disappear. I told him that a local psychic said the house wanted to be presented to me, and that it was meant to be mine. I told him about our strange deal with Mary Wade, and her subsequent warning. He shifted uncomfortably in his chair.

"What do you know about the house? Do you know Mary Wade, do you have a way to contact her? Please, Dr. Lawrence. Something very strange is going on there. I feel like I'm losing my mind. I need your help."

Dr. Lawrence went to the bookcase behind me, removing an entire row of red, leather-bound books with blank spines, stacking them a few at a time on the floor. He placed his hands on the back wall of the empty bookcase section and gently pushed in, popping out the panel. Behind it was an old wooden cigar box. He set the box down on his desk and slid back the lid, pulling out a stack of old, yellowed envelopes bound with twine.

"When I first started teaching at the university about thirty years ago, I found this stack of letters in the antique desk they brought up for me from the basement. They were written in the late 1800s by Eliza Jane Rowe, to her creative writing instructor, Beau Thomas. It seems they were involved romantically, or at least she believed them to be. In these letters, she divulged to him disturbing information about what went on in that family, in that house, and in her own dark, tormented mind."

"Why is there no mention of the letters in your book?"

"The contents of these letters, Miss Farmer, are the ramblings of a young lady suffering from significant mental anguish. These letters should never see the light of day, much less be published."

"I'd like to borrow them, if I may. I promise nothing will happen to them. I won't make copies of them, or show them to anyone else."

"Absolutely not, I'm sorry. They are not to leave my office."

"Could I at least read them? Study them here in your office?"

He thought for a moment. "Very well. You may read them right now, in my presence, just this once." He carefully lifted the stack of letters from the cigar box and set them down gently in front of me. "Be aware, Miss Farmer, that these letters are no doubt perverse distortions of the truth, if there is any truth to them at all. She was, after all, taking a creative writing course."

Dr. Lawrence peeked up from his paperwork every so often, to check the time and see how many letters I had gotten through. He would not permit me to take any notes or photographs, so I used every minute he was willing to give me to commit as much as I could to memory. I knew this chance wouldn't come again. Eliza's letters were dark and powerful. They read more like journal entries than love letters, but instead of Dear Diary, she addressed them to Beau Thomas, the man she loved. In them, Eliza likened herself to Alice in *Alice's Adventures in Wonderland* and *Through the Looking Glass*. I knew these books like the back of my hand; I'd read them both dozens of times, and Amy and I had discussed them at length. They were beyond fascinating.

Alice was a young girl transitioning into womanhood, represented in the book by her becoming queen. She had little to no control over the outcome of her own life, and had very limited exposure to the world outside her home. She was a sad and lonely girl who received very little consideration from those around her. She often fell into despondency, which led her to create a fantastical dream world that was a comprehensive version of her own reality, in order to deal with the anxieties of growing up and the traumas she had faced at an early age. In this dream world, everyone in her immediate life manifested as a character. The only character to show

67

her any compassion was the blue-eyed White Knight, who escorted Alice along her journey to becoming queen, but ultimately left her behind to face her demons alone. Since Alice believed that hardship and loneliness were an inherent part of growing up, even in her fantasy world she forced herself to deal with everything on her own, and under harsh conditions. Alice skillfully blurred the boundaries between her conscious and unconscious mind, so much so, that it became difficult to tell where her reality ended and her dream world began.

I drove home without the comforting accompaniment of an audio book, in favor of reciting aloud everything I could recall reading in Eliza's letters to Beau. I needed to retain as much of them as I possibly could, to burn her words into my mind before they escaped me. I was momentarily amused by the realization that I had just as much trouble keeping words inside my mind as getting them to come out. If these letters were any indication of Eliza's brilliance as a writer, then I was more eager than ever to locate her unfinished manuscript. Perhaps it might inspire me to finally get to work on my own manuscript.

That night, I met Eliza Jane Rowe.

The smell of cedarwood hung in the night air. A pale young woman in a long, gray dress glided past the foot of our bed, her hands clasped neatly in front of her. I sat up in bed and tried to adjust my eyes, sure that I was seeing a roving shadow cast on a piece of furniture by the full moon, until I watched that shadow pivot and make a second pass through the room. She stopped abruptly at the foot of the bed and placed her bony, frail hands on the antique footboard, leaning forward, inserting her face directly into the stream of moonlight coming in from the window. She was both there and not there; tangible, and at the same time, an illusion.

"Elizabeth," she breathed.

"Who are you?" I asked, barely sneaking the question around the large, dry lump that had quickly formed in my throat.

"You know who I am."

I wanted to look away from her, to wake Adam, who was sound asleep right next to me. But I was frozen in place, afraid that if I took my eyes off of her for even a moment, when I looked back toward her again her face would be directly in front of my own, noses end to end, the smell of death escaping from her open mouth and drifting into my own.

"We do look quite similar," she commented. *How could she know I'd had that thought?*

"Why are you here?"

"This is my home, Elizabeth. I have always been here. I will always be here. You did not think I came here just to speak with you, did you?"

"What do you want?"

"I have been watching you, Elizabeth. I have been watching you pretend."

"Pretend what, what am I pretending?"

"Pretending this house belongs to you. Pretending to be any kind of wife. Pretending to be any kind of writer." She stared directly at me as she leaned in, the light tendrils that had come loose from her pinned back hair were swaying in front of her face as she breathed, her skin as dull and gray as the dress she wore. "You seek the truth, and so I will give it to you myself," she declared. "Dr. Lawrence is a useless man, and you are wasting valuable time."

She moved to the side of the bed and flung the covers from me, grabbing the wrist of my right hand that was clutching the edge of the mattress, and pulling me to my feet. Her hands were scaly and frigid. She dragged me into the corridor and down the main upstairs hallway, to one of the spare bedrooms near the top of the stairs. She stood in the doorway, pointing to the cedar hope chest at the foot of the bed. I walked to it and knelt down in front of it. I slid the metal latch to the side and pushed open the heavy lid. The smell of cedarwood consumed the stale air inside the stuffy, closed off room.

The chest was full, and laying across the top was a haggard old doll in a pristine white christening gown. I grabbed the doll around her soft, batting-filled body that was covered in a flour sack material and lifted it from the trunk, her eyelids clanking open as I tilted her upright. Her painted porcelain face was cracked down the center, one of her eyes was missing, and something was rattling around inside of her hollow head.

"Her name is Mary Ellen…"

Ethan and Eliza

Eliza's older brother Ethan was incredibly smart and good looking. He was always the best and most popular student, and was noticeably favored by Mr. and Mrs. Rowe. No one but Eliza knew that Ethan was a very disturbed young man who took great joy in torturing his sister.

In their younger years, he caught spiders and put them in her hair on the walk to school, so he could enjoy watching her scream and claw at her head in fear. Sometimes, if he was lucky enough to find one, he would pick up a grass snake and throw it onto her shoulders. When they arrived at school and everyone quickly noticed Eliza's unkempt appearance, Ethan told their classmates she refused to bathe or comb her hair. When the teacher inquired about the scratches on her face, Ethan told her Eliza had done it to herself. Technically speaking, it was the truth. Eliza longed to tell someone what was happening to her, but Ethan had swung her favorite doll, Mary Ellen, against a tree, cracking her face down the center and dislodging one of her beautiful blue eyes from its socket, sending it inside of her hollow head. Ethan promised to do the same thing to Eliza, if she ever told a soul.

As they got older, Ethan became much crueler. Eliza started losing her hair due to stress and anxiety. She began pulling it back into a very tight bun each day, to protect against her brother, as well as to disguise her increasing baldness. She took one of her mother's empty perfume bottles and made herself a fragranced concoction using lily of the valley she found growing wild where the edge of the garden met the neighboring woods. She thought if she smelled nice, no one would believe she didn't bathe. When Ethan realized this, he emptied the bottle and replaced it with insecticide, causing her nausea, headaches, and a severe skin reaction on her chest, neck, and wrists. As she rubbed at her inflamed skin, it became more irritated and began to spread across her body.

This is when Eliza Rowe, much to her mother's pleasant surprise, took up an interest in sewing. But the first time Eliza came down the stairs wearing a dreadful patchwork of fabrics she'd cut from her dresses and pieced together to cover every possible inch of her body, her mother nearly fainted at the sight. Eliza was on the verge of heat stroke every time she walked to school or did her chores in one of these hooded, full-body garments. Not to mention, her new fashion sense provided Ethan and their classmates with additional fodder for her ridicule.

Ethan smiled through dinner every evening, as Eliza pushed and combed through her food, examining it for whatever he might have done to it. Their mother delighted in Ethan's handsome grin, and disparaged Eliza for not being a more gracious recipient of their bounty. Soon she stopped showing up to the dinner table altogether, claiming to be ill. She ate alone in her room, things that she had tucked into her dress pockets while helping her mother in the gardens after school. Things she knew were fresh and untampered with. A few small vegetables, a few berries, and the sweet-smelling lily of the valley she'd become so fond of. She began to shed weight that her already frail figure could not afford to lose, in part due to the frequent vomiting that was no doubt caused by her terribly frayed nerves.

Eliza began pushing her desk in front of her bedroom door at night, after seeing her doorknob move a time or two, directly following quieted footsteps in the hallway. It could very well have been her mother or father coming to look in on her, but in her mind, it was always Ethan, preparing for his next torturous game. The wall between their bedrooms seemed to weaken and thin as the months passed. Sometimes as she laid in bed listening to Ethan incessantly bang against their common wall, she was certain it was bending, reaching out for her with every knock, convinced that one day the wall would stretch far enough to grab her by the throat. Even the walls seemed to be on Ethan's side.

Her journals were her only confidante, and she wrote feverishly for many hours every night. She couldn't bear to write about what was truly happening to her, so she escaped by writing fantastical, fictional stories loosely based on the truth. One of her other late-night activities was to quietly work at prying up a few of the floorboards where her desk belonged, so when it was back in place during the day, her writings were hidden safely underneath. While other girls her age were likely collecting pretty rocks and trinkets, Eliza collected the crooked nails from her floorboards, and hid them in a spice tin underneath her mattress. Sometimes she would take them out and look them over, carefully choosing one to fantasize about plunging into Ethan's neck.

In her closet, she kept a large canning jar she'd taken from the kitchen. This kept her from having to leave her room at night once her parents were asleep. When the jar was nearly full with urine, she would pour it out her bedroom window. This kept Ethan from tripping her, scaring her, or locking the door behind her on late night trips to the outhouse.

A few long years later, Ethan graduated and left the peninsula to attend medical school in California. There were certainly medical schools much nearer to home, but Ethan seized the opportunity to see as much of America as he could along the way. Eliza became a lovely young woman, flourishing in his absence. She was still living with her parents, taking a creative writing class at the new university that had just been opened, and was about to marry her literature professor, Beau Thomas. Her hair grew back and her skin recovered, but she still wore her unusual handmade garments, with long sleeves and high necks, no matter the season, to hide the many ugly scars Ethan left her with. Beau hadn't seen her scars, though she told him all about them, and all about what Ethan had done to her. She couldn't bear to speak her truth, so she wrote it all to him in letters, which she tucked into the pages of her weekly writing assignments.

Beau Thomas was a literary scholar visiting from New York City, an interim professor covering the medical leave of the usual creative writing instructor. He wasn't tall or strong, but he was reliable. He wasn't very good looking, but he had kind eyes and good manners. He was exactly what Eliza needed. Beau kept her night table well stocked with wonderful books, and they spent hours discussing them, as well as her writing. Beau believed in her, and he had access to publishers, to editors. She was going to be a published author, Beau would see to it, and together they would return to New York City when his tenure came to a close. What a dream come true it would be, to be a husband-and-wife team, living and working together in the most exciting city imaginable. They would be married just as soon as the school term ended.

Ethan became a doctor, which he claimed was a desire born from seeing his sister unwell most of her life. He lived across the country in California with his new wife, Isabelle, and his letters home indicated they were expecting their first child. Mr. and Mrs. Rowe made the long journey to Ethan's wedding, of course, but Eliza said she was ill so she wouldn't have to accompany them. Though her good health had returned, she remained ill in a way, sickened by the thought of how many people Ethan could be torturing in her absence. Was he a good doctor? Was he a good husband? Would he be a good father? Had he become a good man, and if so, did he deserve to be forgiven for the terrors he'd caused her as a boy?

There was simply no way to get around Ethan and his wife attending Eliza's wedding to Beau after church on Sunday morning. Eliza peeked out the front parlor window, through the inch of curtain she held back, standing off to the side so Ethan didn't catch her watching them arrive that Saturday afternoon. Mrs. Rowe said she was going to wear a hole in the floor, as often as she stood in that spot by the parlor window. Isabelle was stunning, Eliza noticed, as she watched Ethan dote on his pregnant bride while he unloaded their bags and ushered her toward the front door. Mr. and Mrs. Rowe were beyond delighted to see them. The four had exchanged embraces and greetings, then Ethan spotted Eliza by the parlor window and came toward her, smiling. Eliza froze with fear.

"You are looking well, Eliza," Ethan said with a smile, as he approached her with his arms outstretched. Eliza declined to meet his embrace. "I would like you to meet my wife, Isabelle." Isabelle waddled toward them, her hands cradling her very pregnant stomach.

"It is so nice to finally meet you, Eliza. Ethan has told me so much about you." Dear God, Eliza thought. Did Isabelle know everything Ethan had done to her? The nervous and frightened look on her face suggested that she must.

"Congratulations," Eliza said quickly, and with well-hidden insincerity.

They entered the dining room for their evening meal just as Beau arrived at the house. He quietly slipped himself into the empty chair beside Eliza and took her hand beneath the table. Nobody noticed. Beau knew she must have been panicking inside with Ethan seated across from her again, after so much time had passed. The dinner conversation at first focused on talk of the baby, then quickly turned to Eliza, who hated being the center of attention. Her family lovingly told every funny and strange story they had of her – from her refusal to bathe or brush her hair as a girl, to the time she smashed her favorite doll against a tree, to her fear of using the outhouse after dark, to the many meals she refused to eat. They were careful not to mention her unusual handmade garments, as she was still in the habit of wearing them. Plates were passed, endearing tales were told, and many laughs were shared, as if Eliza had simply been a quirky and impetuous child with a wild imagination and a gift for storytelling.

"I admit to scaring her with a harmless grass snake now and then," Ethan stated with unbelievable charm. "As is every big brother's right. But I always took good care of her," Ethan turned to his wife and smiled, leaning over to lovingly kiss the top of her head.

Eliza helped her mother and Isabelle clear the dinner table as Beau silently followed Mr. Rowe and Ethan outside for a cigar on the front porch before heading back to the boarding house. All was quiet that night. No one tried to enter her room. The walls maintained their original posture.

The family was early to church on Sunday morning. Eliza wore her mother's wedding dress, which she had reconstructed to cover her entire body, of course. The podium and chairs were in place, and everything was perfect. The wedding was to follow the morning sermon, but as it drew to a close, Beau was still not there.

"Finally, let us pray for our dear friend Beau Thomas," the reverend spoke, "who completed his tenure here with us this week, and boarded the Saturday afternoon train back to New York City. We thank the good Lord for his service to us. May his travels be safe and his future be bright."

"What have you done?" Eliza yelled, springing from her seat and towering over Ethan. "He can't be gone. He would never willingly leave without me!" Eliza burst into tears.

"Please don't cry," Ethan said calmly, quietly. "I'll try to find him for you."

Mr. and Mrs. Rowe quickly escorted Eliza from the church with Isabelle in tow, mortified by the eruption the whole congregation had just witnessed. Ethan returned to the house that afternoon. Eliza could hear him speaking from her room, where she laid on the bed, her face tacky from hours of crying, clutching her spice tin of crooked nails to her chest. Ethan informed his wife and parents of Beau's empty room at the boarding house. His classroom was empty as well, neat and clean, the only trace of his presence there being a bound stack of letters from Eliza, left in the drawer of his desk.

In that moment, it became clear to Eliza that Ethan had done something to Beau, and he had offered to search for him in an effort to divert suspicion. He must have slipped away that night and hurt him, or killed him, or at the very least threatened to do to him what he had done to Mary Ellen, if he didn't leave town immediately. That is why all was quiet at home, she thought. Not because Ethan was in any way a changed man, but because he was too busy sabotaging her only chance at a happy and successful life away from this place. The only home she'd ever known. A place she now loved and hated with equal measure.

Still in her mother's wedding dress, Eliza sprung from her bed, whipped open her bedroom door, flew down the stairs, and charged at Ethan. The unsettling sound of pure rage projected from Eliza Rowe's throat as she plunged a crooked nail into her brother's neck.

Isabelle laid awake that night in pure shock, unable to ignore the sound of hammering and sawing coming from the main barn as Mr. Rowe constructed a casket for his only son. Mrs. Rowe sobbed through the night, as she worked feverishly to scrub Ethan's blood from the parlor floor. She insisted on a formal and proper presentation, under any and all circumstances. Eliza slept better than she ever had.

Ethan's casket was placed in the ground at sunrise. Isabelle, terrified and bereaved, started the journey back to California immediately following the graveside prayer, despite Mr. and Mrs. Rowe pleading with her to stay with them, so that they could help her to raise their grandchild. Isabelle wanted nothing to do with the Rowe family, and vowed never to return to the Rowe farm, but agreed to accept a monthly stipend in exchange for her cooperation. She was simply to tell people there had been an unexpected incident during their trip to visit Ethan's childhood home, that private family services were held, and that Ethan was buried in the family plot. Technically speaking, it was the truth.

Mr. Rowe enlisted the help of his most trusted farmhand, John Freeman, to build a simple but beautiful cottage on the other side of the woods, next to the creek at the edge of the property line. Eliza viewed the cottage as a glorious reward she greatly deserved, after suffering through so many years of torment and injustice. She had everything she needed, and everything had a place. She did not see the cottage as the punishment and banishment it was intended to be. There was no need to lock her inside, she didn't have any desire to leave the cottage or return to the farm, and she was certain if she did, Ethan's ghost would be waiting for her in the woods, along with the spiders and the snakes.

Her father never saw or spoke to her again. Her mother visited daily at first, then weekly, then not at all. John's wife, Jenny, who also lived and worked on the Rowe farm, delivered baked goods, sundries, and fresh writing materials to the cottage every few days. Occasionally, a new book to read. Jenny also made sure there was an ample supply of berries, wild mushrooms and asparagus, and edible plants and flowers growing right outside her door. No living creature deserved less. Eliza stayed there, alone, reading and writing diligently, until she succumbed to her unknown ailments. She was bathed. Her hair was brushed and pulled back tightly into a neat bun. She was placed in a simple gray dress that her mother chose for her.

Her body had no scars.

The Cottage

I flew out of bed, into the corridor, and down the main upstairs hallway, to the still opened door of the bedroom I now knew used to belong to Eliza Jane Rowe. The room I had closed the door to when we first moved into the house, because it gave me such an unsettling feeling. The cedar chest at the foot of the bed was still open, and the doll, Mary Ellen, was laying on the floor just where I had placed her, in what could not have been a dream. I knelt down next to her and began to look through the rest of the trunk. There they were, folded neatly in three equal stacks across the top – Eliza's unusual, full-body garments. I ran my fingers over the seams, and swore I could feel her suffering embedded into each and every stitch. Something was tucked safely inside the final dress. I unfolded it slowly. It was the perfume bottle, cut crystal with gold fittings, and an atomizer bulb with an intricately crocheted overlay. The liquid inside had long been evaporated, leaving a light amber-colored stain inside part of the orb. The rest of the chest contained random childhood keepsakes. No spice tin full of crooked nails. No canning jar. No journals, and no manuscript.

"Good morning," Adam was leaning against the door frame in his blue plaid boxer shorts, a fresh white towel slung over his shoulder. "What are you doing in here?"

"You startled me," I said. "Good morning. Just looking for an extra throw blanket. I thought I might write outside on the porch this morning." *Lie.*

"The picnic blanket is in the back of the Jeep. I'll set it on the porch before I head to the office."

"Thanks," I smiled.

Adam continued down the hallway to the bathroom. I quickly ran my hands along every inch of the cedar chest, looking for some kind of hidden compartment where the manuscript might be. I carefully placed each item back in the chest, exactly as it had been, closed the lid, and latched it. I shut the bedroom door behind me.

It was unclear to me exactly what I had experienced the night before. There was no mention of the cottage in anything I had read about the Rowe farm, and it was not mentioned in Dr. Lawrence's book. The doll and the perfume bottle actually existed. I needed to find out if the cottage did too. I watched from the front parlor window as Adam took the picnic blanket from the Jeep and set it on the porch swing for me, before leaving for work. I stood there for a moment, imagining Eliza standing in the very same spot, watching Ethan and Isabelle arrive. I could feel the anguish she must have felt in that moment, as she observed her tormentor's return.

The creak in the floorboards directly beneath where I stood, where Eliza had once stood, ripped her from the past and placed her front and center in my reality, so firmly that I half expected her to reach up through the wooden planks and grab me by the ankle. I stood there examining every detail of the room, every piece of furniture, every decoration, wondering what would have been in Ethan's frame of view, as he laid there bleeding to death on the parlor floor.

Without taking the time to bathe or brush my hair, I threw on the clothes nearest to me, filled a travel mug with coffee, and grabbed my book bag. The kitchen screen door thwapped behind me as I hurried down the porch steps and made my way to the fieldstone footpath leading into the woods. If there truly was a cottage out there, and I knew there had to be, this was the most logical path to it.

The trail became less and less manicured as I descended deeper into the woods. Specks of sunlight peeking through the treetops created a lace of moving shadows on the uneven ground. The trees were an eclectic mix of tall, old hardwoods, not unlike one of Eliza's unusual patchwork garments. Oaks, cedars, black walnuts, and maples, dispersed among a sea of pines.

So girl, my girl, don't lie to me.
Girl, please don't tell me why.
Girl, my girl, don't tear my heart out,
but where did you sleep last night?
Pines, in the pines,
where the sun don't ever shine,
Pines, in the pines,
where I choose to spend my time.

The tree roots wove in and out of the ground as they slithered away from their trunks. I spotted several varieties of wild mushrooms – some edible, some poisonous, and one I believed to be psychotropic. The forest floor was crawling with toxic, parasitic ghost pipe, also known as corpse flower. If these were the kind of things Eliza had been eating, no wonder she was so sick. I heard the reliable hum of tree frogs, which told me there were also snakes lurking nearby. I felt like something was resting on my shoulders, immediately picturing Ethan behind me, grinning and holding a grass snake. It was just my own messy hair, which I quickly remedied by pulling it back into a tight bun. There was a clearing ahead where the sun could beam down, next to a beautiful creek with lily of the valley growing along the edge. Deceptively pretty and sweet, lily of the valley could stop your heart if ingested in large enough quantity.

There it was.

The cottage was barely visible, seated in the center of a massive nest of overgrowth, with ugly, thorny vines wrapping around it, like a thick barbed wire surrounding a prison. There was no way I could have known it was here, or seen it from the main house. I felt my body swaying back and forth, as I worked up the nerve to fight my way through the immense overgrowth. I stomped down the invasive brush, bending it away from me as I clawed through the mass of dense plants and vines, which supported and strangled one other simultaneously. Half of it was alive and well, and half of it was long dead, yet they worked seamlessly together toward their common goal. I pulled my sleeves down over my hands for a slight amount of protection as I continued to snap and pull through the mass, while it pierced and clawed into my skin. Eventually, I reached the cottage door.

Stepping forward into the cottage felt like stepping backward through time. The interior of the cottage was clad with cedar boards, with a beamed framework supporting the roof. There was a cast iron stove in the middle of the room, which served as a heat source, as well as a place to boil water or heat food. A cauldron-style pot and a kettle sat beside it. A single bed stood in the corner next to the back door, which was directly across from the front door. There would be no need for two entrances on a house this small, so it must have been for the purpose of aeration. A small wooden table was pushed against the wall under the window, with a matching wooden chair tucked underneath each end. An upholstered arm chair and a small side table were angled in the final corner. Just like the main house, it had absolutely no right to be in such pristine condition for its age. There wasn't a speck of dust or a trace of infestation. Everything was clean, dry, and like new.

All four walls, from floor to ceiling, were lined with bookshelves that were filled with books. Painted, written, and carved into every available surface of the interior were words. Sentences. Poems. Passages. It was like walking around inside of a book. No, it was like walking around inside of Eliza Rowe's mind. I pulled my phone from my book bag and photographed every inch of the interior. While zooming in, I noticed a row of very old, very valuable first editions, published in the late 1800s. Dickens. Dostoyevsky. Tolstoy. Verne. And the crown jewels: *Alice's Adventures in Wonderland* and *Through the Looking Glass* by Lewis Carroll, published in 1865 and 1871, respectively. A quote from Carroll was scratched into the wood beneath them.

"There are skeptical thoughts, which seem for the moment to uproot the firmest faith; there are blasphemous thoughts, which dart unbidden into the most reverent souls; there are unholy thoughts, which torture, with their hateful presence, the fancy that would fain be pure. Against all these some real mental work is a most helpful ally."

It was an early Christian belief that the devil could skillfully slip into idle, vulnerable minds. Lewis Carroll, whose given name was Charles Dodgson, journaled all of his adult life, presumably for the purpose of preventing his mind from being commandeered by the devil. Perhaps Eliza wrote incessantly to keep her own mind from being commandeered. Perhaps Eliza and the Rowe farm could not be so cruel to me if I were only writing myself.

I told myself that as an unyielding lover of literature and history, I could no way in good conscience leave these priceless first editions out here in the woods for just anyone to stumble onto. I mean, I bought the property and all its contents, right? Technically, they belonged to me. I put them in my book bag and took one last look around the cottage for Eliza's unfinished manuscript. I did my best to secure the cottage door, and then started back through the woods to the house. My chest, neck, and wrists began to itch. I carefully hid the first editions behind some other books in the study and stood there for a moment, scanning the bookcase. *Where was Eliza's unfinished manuscript?* It had to be somewhere on the property. I went upstairs to shower, change my clothes, and pull myself together before Adam came home. As I rubbed at my inflamed skin it became more irritated, and began to spread across my body.

"Hey, how was your day?" Adam came through the kitchen door as I was making dinner. I didn't leave myself a lot of time, so I boiled some penne pasta and quickly sautéed it with olive oil, garlic, and whatever leftovers I could find in the fridge.

"Hey. Good, how was yours?"

"Good," he smiled. "It smells great in here."

He came around the side of the kitchen island to set down his things and kiss me on the cheek, immediately noticing my red, inflamed skin. He gently took my face in his hands and held it under the light to get a better look.

"What were you doing in the woods today?"

"I took a walk." Technically speaking, it was the truth. "How did you know?"

"You're covered in poison oak."

John and Jenny

The 13th Amendment to the Constitution abolished slavery and all other iterations of involuntary servitude in the United States in late 1865. For the majority of African Americans, this brought an end to the brutalities and indignities of slave life – the whippings and sexual assaults, the selling and forcible relocation of family members, and the denial of education, legal marriage, and the ownership of property. While many former slaves (who were given new first names by their owners upon arrival in America) took the surnames of their last owner upon being freed, John decided his surname would literally be free man.

John Freeman was the best farmhand there was. Actually, John was the best at everything. Upon receiving his freedom, he had offers from multiple landowners who would have offered anything to retain him, but John Freeman made the choice to travel from North Carolina to New York all on his own, working long and hard for anyone willing to provide him with a simple meal and a place to sleep along the way. There was only one reason a newly-freed black man would travel alone, on foot, across a country that wasn't ready to embrace him.

Love.

John met Jenny in 1860 aboard a ship called The Constantine, which had illegally trafficked a small selection of elite African-descended captives into the United States. Aboard this same ship were a few wealthy and powerful individuals from unknown European origins, who went to great lengths to connect with the crew of The Constantine and arrange secret entrance into the United States. Among those passengers were Mr. and Mrs. Rowe.

John had been custom ordered like a piece of fine furniture, by a wealthy North Carolina man in the building trade, who paid handsomely to acquire his elaborate skill set. Only a select number of the country's finest families were made aware of The Constantine's efforts, and many traveled for weeks to meet up with the ship and claim their orders. John and Jenny said goodbye with their eyes, as Jenny was removed from the ship in New York, and John continued on to his purchaser in North Carolina. In addition to John, he had ordered large quantities of rare and precious metals, stones, and woods from around the world. He was determined to make a fortune building and selling the grandest, most unique homes in all of America.

It was assumed that Jenny was the worthless young daughter of a very valuable African woman with unmatched culinary talents. The woman would be staying in New York City to cook for an American business magnate who built his wealth in railroads and shipping, and was the man behind The Constantine's secret deliveries. With the woman supposedly came many unusual spices, herbs, seeds, and oils from remote corners of the globe, however, when the woman was delivered, those items were nowhere to be found. Jenny was taken from the woman thought to be her mother as soon as they arrived in New York, and was placed with a small group of other discarded individuals to be sold cheaply on sight at the docks. The proceeds of the on-sight sales were always given back to the crew of The Constantine, to guarantee their continued efforts and ensure their discretion. Jenny was purchased by Mr. and Mrs. Rowe, who knew she was far from worthless.

Aboard the ship, Mr. and Mrs. Rowe heard the crew of The Constantine contemplate entering New York at its northernmost peninsula, instead of the bustling New York Harbor, and making the rest of the journey to New York City by land. However, after recounting what they knew of the area's harsh, rocky terrain, lack of resources, and unpredictable weather, the crew decided it wasn't worth the added risk. Mr. and Mrs. Rowe decided in that moment that upon arriving in New York Harbor, they would travel by land to the northernmost peninsula and make their new home in the area widely thought to be so uninhabitable. For the next five years, Jenny lived and worked alongside Mr. and Mrs. Rowe as they built a life for themselves in the newly-formed town of Haven. She was like a daughter to them. When slavery ended in 1865, Jenny took the surname Rowe with their eager encouragement.

Everyone in Haven believed that Jenny was a witch. They weren't wrong. Jenny came from a long line of witches, shamans, midwives, and soothsayers. She had many incredible gifts, including the ability to speak to the dead and predict the future. Sometimes, the dead came through her, delivering messages from beyond the grave. These messages were often received abruptly, or at inopportune moments, and could be an embarrassment for the recipient. For this reason, some people avoided Jenny when she came into town. Others avoided her because she was different, or simply because they could sense how powerful she was – and it terrified them. Despite her talent and power, Jenny was as kind and courteous as a person could possibly be, generous with her time and gifts, and always the first person to offer her assistance to someone in need.

A man by the name of John Bentley Kingston, a well-known Spiritualist leader, traveled to Haven all the way from Salem, Massachusetts to meet the young girl he'd heard could speak to the dead. Among the Spiritualist belief system was the idea that spirits lived closer to God, so communicating with them could help the living to understand God's purpose for them. Spiritualism was sweeping the country, and Kingston believed it was his purpose to further it by opening a Spiritualist school. He hoped Jenny could ask the spirits how he might best acquire the funding for his school in Salem. Jenny urged him to purchase a specific piece of land on the peninsula. He did, and the mining of that land gave Kingston all the capital he needed to open his school. Jenny also urged him to open his school on the peninsula instead. In gratitude for the good fortune she'd brought to him, he obliged.

People gathered in small, private groups in the evenings to hold séances. Some gathered in the parlors of their homes, others chose to use the séance rooms at Kingston's new school. Some groups held hands, while others placed their palms flat on the table. Some groups remained silent, while others were prone to hysterics. Some truly believed they were about to receive messages from another realm, while others were quite simply there to be entertained. Whatever the case, the common denominator was always Jenny.

Spiritualism gave closure and comfort to the bereaved, and offered the assurance of an afterlife to help support the growing uncertainties of the Christian faith. It was believed that young girls transitioning into womanhood were the perfect vessels for this kind of mediumship. That, combined with her mysterious talents and unknown origins, made a once seemingly worthless girl a very priceless commodity.

Jenny always knew that John would eventually come for her, and cast a spell to ensure his safety until then. She knew the moment they met on the ship, that one day they would be together. That was, Sarah told me, how soul mates worked. The Rowes had always been prepared to take John in when that day came. Construction began on the smaller farmhouse positioned just off the main road as soon as the land purchase was complete. Mr. and Mrs. Rowe trusted Jenny completely when she urged them to purchase the barren land that was Haven Hill. Mr. Rowe had a decent skill set of his own, and he hired a competent crew to assist him. When John arrived in 1865, construction of the main house began.

John and Jenny married immediately, and were beyond happy. Once the main house was habitable, Mr. and Mrs. Rowe settled in and gifted the smaller farmhouse to John and Jenny, along with a bit of land that Mr. Rowe signed over to them as a wedding gift. They were the gatekeepers of the property. They worked alongside Mr. and Mrs. Rowe every single day, and earned a very respectable wage, but they were not employees. They were family. That year, Mr. and Mrs. Rowe welcomed a son, who they named Ethan. John continued to add more and more rooms to the main house, for all the children Mr. and Mrs. Rowe intended to have. It was their greatest dream that generations of Rowes would always have this sacred, protected homestead where they would raise their families and live their lives together.

While John knew exactly how to build a solid structure that would stand the test of time, Jenny knew exactly how to make sure that structure was properly communing with the natural world. She knew how to coexist with the wildlife, appease the elements, and harness atmospheric energy. She knew how to respectfully harvest the plant life without harm or waste. She knew how to cultivate the proper environment for resurrection. They took the lives of animals only when absolutely necessary, and were sure to use every aspect of the kill. They protected animal young, and they never separated families. No living creature deserved less. Jenny understood that our relationships with other living things was not only fundamental to our survival, but the benchmark of our humanity.

John hand built the flagstone paths that traveled from the kitchen door of the main house, to their house, to the woods, and to the creek. The creek ran parallel to Haven Hill, and indicated the end of the Rowe property line. Jenny placed cairns in all four corners of the property, each paying respect to one of the four basal elements – earth, air, fire, and water. On the night of every new moon, John would accompany Jenny to each of the four corners and stand watch while she made an offering to the elements and placed a blessing on the property that it would continue to flourish, as long as all things within it were respected and revered. This blessing was accompanied equally by a curse, that if this standard of care was not upheld, the infraction would be met with swift retribution.

There were many commonalities between Spiritualism and the more mainstream Christian faiths of the time. Particularly, the interpretation of the fragile relationship between obedience and disobedience, and the very fine line between a blessing and a curse. The book of Deuteronomy outlines what all faiths have some iteration of, that an unseen higher power, whatever or whoever that may be, will rain blessings upon those who live with respect and grace. Those who are disrespectful, or fall from grace, would be flooded by curse. With Jenny's guidance, Kingston created his own version of Deuteronomy, partnered with Spiritualism, and governed by his personal beliefs surrounding knowledge, purpose, morality, and judgement. Jenny took Kingston's Law one step further, by using her supernatural powers to sear it directly into the Rowe farm.

Kingston's Law

Blessings for Obedience:

- If you carefully listen to the land and do as it requires, you will be placed high above all others. You will be blessed upon the land as well as when away, given your promise to return and to charge only the worthy with its care.
- Your children will be plenty, and each blessed with optimal physical, mental, and emotional health.
- Your basket and your kneading trough will be blessed. Your crops and your livestock will be plentiful, by understanding that our role is not to dominate other life, but to properly honor and commune with it.
- Any enemies who dare rise up against you will be defeated before you. They will come at you from one direction, but flee from you in four.

- Everything you put your hand to will be blessed. Your land will flourish, your animals will thrive, your buildings will be sturdy and sound. Your people and your land will be fertile.
- You will be granted abundant prosperity, for yourselves and all your ancestors to come. You will be pillars of your community, and of your church. You will lend to many, but will borrow from none.
- The heavens, the storehouse of bounty, will open for you. You will always be at the top, never at the bottom.

Curses for Disobedience:

- If you fail to carefully listen to the land and do as it requires, you will be promptly placed below all others. You will be cursed upon the land, as well as when away. There will be no place of respite for you.
- You will bear no children, and those children you have already been blessed with will suffer tremendous physical, mental, and emotional deterioration. They will experience crippling madness and confusion. They will be plagued with an anxious mind, eyes weary with longing, and a despairing heart.
- Your basket will burn and your kneading trough will crack. Your crops and your livestock will die off, but not before turning on you.
- Any enemies who dare rise up against you will quickly defeat you. They will come at you from all directions, leaving you with no path to flee from.
- Everything you put your hand to will be cursed. Your land will waste away, your animals will fail to thrive, your buildings will tilt, crumble, and burn. Your people and your land will be barren.
- You will be weighted with financial burden, for yourselves and all your ancestors to come. You will be outcasts of your community, and of your church. You will become a thing of horror, and an object of ridicule. You will seek mercy, but none will be offered.
- The heavens, the storehouse of bounty, will close to you. You will always be at the bottom, never at the top.

Kingston University

I applied for the master's degree program at Kingston University. The fall semester had already begun, but a personal letter of recommendation – and the promise of a guest lecture – from best-selling, Nobel prize-winning author Margaret Fuller was more than enough to secure a late admission. Margaret gave me until the time of her guest lecture to have the first draft of my manuscript completed. That was a reasonable amount of time, since she was under the impression I'd been writing since we arrived in Haven. It was not a reasonable amount of time, however, for me to write an entire novel from concept to completion, which was what I actually had to do. At this point, my only hope of meeting this deadline was to locate Eliza's unfinished manuscript and pray to God I could use it.

Margaret connected me with a friend of hers in the Sotheby's Books and Manuscripts department, who had no trouble orchestrating the quick and private sale of one of the first editions I found in the cottage. With that sale, I was able to cover my tuition in full, buy myself a car to get to and from campus, and replenish the funds we'd used to purchase the doctor's office. Adam was very supportive of my plans. I told him about the first editions, but allowed him to assume I had found them in the study, telling him nothing of the cottage in the woods. He simply thought luck was once again on our side, and was thrilled that everything was finally coming together for us both. He had his own private practice and at very young age, I was in graduate school and writing, we had a beautiful home full of valuable assets, and we were ready to start a family.

We were going to have it all.

The Master of Arts in Literature program was an incredible intellectual challenge. It required analyzing complex information, challenging established assumptions, pondering competing considerations, and reaching effective conclusions – all of which were of secondary use to me. What I needed now was a crash course in all things spiritual and supernatural.

Sarah.

✟

"Old scar face is right. The property has never been sold, and it has never left the Rowe family. It never can, and it never will. You are a Rowe, Elizabeth Farmer. I helped Mary find you, bring you here, and present the house to you."

"That's ridiculous. I would know if I had family in this area. I would have heard stories about this place."

"It's true. Ethan Rowe and his wife, Isabelle Merrick, had a daughter. She named her Anne Elizabeth Merrick. Isabelle raised her in California after Ethan's death. She never told Anne about the Rowe family, or this property. Anne married Hudson St. Clair, and they had a daughter named Helen. Helen St. Clair moved to New York and married…"

"Jack Farmer," I mumbled. My father. "Why would you bring me into all this? How could you do that to me?"

"We didn't do it *to* you, we did it *for* you! You needed this. I'm sorry, Elizabeth Farmer, but your life was going nowhere. We gave you everything you'd ever dreamed of," she laughed.

"Why me? Why not someone else in my family?"

"Mary was the last Rowe raised here, so we had to look to Isabelle's line. You, your mother, and your sister were the closest geographically, so we started there. When we learned you were an aspiring writer and your husband a doctor, well it couldn't have been more perfect."

"What about Mary's daughter? And if the property has to be continually passed down, what was the fifty thousand dollars for?"

"Mary is dying. She's in a hospice facility in Bennington, Vermont. You paid for that. Dr. Whitmore took her there, and then he retired to Florida to be with his daughter. Mary borrowed his story. I'm sorry we lied to you, but she was running out of time. She couldn't die here."

"Why? What is this place?"

"Do you know what a nexus is, Elizabeth Farmer?" I shook my head, no. "It's a point of incredible energy equidistant from five significant points, forming a pentagram. Exactly in the center of those points is Haven Hill, and at the top of the hill sits…"

"My house."

"Environmental energy constantly surrounds us, but it's especially concentrated on ley lines. Ley lines crisscross around the globe, and are littered with powerful monuments and natural landforms, and carry along with them rivers of supernatural energy. Along these lines, at the places they intersect, there are pockets of concentrated energy, that can be harnessed only by spirits and spiritual individuals.

Whoever controls this property, controls the power of the nexus. That's why the Rowes have never let it leave their family, and pass down the cautionary words you received from Mary. The slightest indiscretion can tip the scales. What Eliza did, killing her brother, it tipped the scales significantly. It took generations to make it right. The spiritual laws that govern this land don't make exceptions for the mentally unstable.

Jenny knew exactly what she was doing when she urged the original Rowe family to build on Haven Hill. She was smart and gifted, but also young and unguided. She didn't realize the eternal burden she would be placing on the Rowe family when she cast her spell on the land within the nexus. She didn't realize she would be tethering all their souls here to uphold her words."

"I don't understand why Mary didn't just sell something to pay for her care. The house is full of valuable things. We liquidated nearly everything we had to come up with that fifty thousand."

"Didn't Mary tell you that everything stays with the house?"

"She did, but that's what people always say when they're selling a furnished house."

"Oh no. Please tell me you didn't…"

I did. Margaret's friend from the Sotheby's Books and Manuscripts Department drove all the way here from New York City and retrieved the book herself. She handed me the check personally, after having me sign a very lengthy release form. I was curious, of course, who had purchased the book and where it would be going, but she informed me that Sotheby's prided itself on the strictest confidentiality. She did say what an exciting transaction it was, as this buyer had been looking for this particular first edition for several decades.

"I know who the buyer is," Sarah laughed. "I know where the book is, and we have to get it back."

"I can't buy it back, Sarah. The money has already been spent."

"I didn't say *buy* it back, Elizabeth Farmer. I said *get* it back."

At first glance, South Haven seemed like nothing more than a sleepy little college town. I quickly discovered it was anything but. "Kingston University was originally founded for the study of Spiritualism," Sarah started. "That brought Spiritualists here from all over the country, to settle in an area previously rooted in Christianity. It's what brought my mother's family here. It was all just Haven, once, until it became divided by religion. Spiritualism can still be studied here, but more so in theory, as part of a degree in theology, philosophy, or comparative religion. The school was modernized in the 1940s after the founder's death, when they added mainstream courses of study in order to keep the doors open."

"It seems strange to choose such a Christian location for a Spiritualist school."

"The story is that Kingston traveled here to see a young psychic medium, hoping to ask the spirits for guidance in opening a Spiritualist school in Salem, Massachusetts. Instead, she urged him to buy a specific piece of land here in Haven. He didn't understand, but listened, and that land turned out to hold some of the richest iron ore in the state. Kingston became incredibly wealthy, and decided to give back to the area that gave him his fortune, so he opened his school here instead. That's how North Haven got the nickname Second Salem. Well, that and all the witches," she laughed.

"Witches?"

"When the school modernized, most of the real Spiritualist study went underground…literally. There's a system of caverns beneath the peninsula, created ages ago by icebergs passing below. They gathered dust for several decades, until they were utilized to keep Kingston's teachings in practice after the modernization, when Christianity reclaimed the area. Anyone believed to be practicing Spiritualism or Kingston's Law after the reclaiming was labeled a witch."

Melinda Marin dreamed of attending Kingston University, just as her parents had. She prepared for it all her life. The one thing Melinda hadn't been prepared for was falling in love with her literature professor. He was fascinating, worldly, and nearly twice her age. She was young, beautiful, and naïve. By the time Melinda discovered what kind of a man Dr. Stephen Lawrence truly was, she was already carrying his child.

Dr. Lawrence planned to propose to Melinda in the most sacred place in the world to him – the secret archive room beneath the basement of the Kingston University library. Collected over the course of two hundred years, the materials housed in the secret archive included: rare books, documents, letters, famous works of art, photographs, drawings, paintings, blueprints, ledgers, religious artifacts, and recordings on film, tape, and video. These materials documented everything John Bentley Kingston and his followers had ever done in the name of advancing his iteration of Spiritualism.

The basement of the library housed rows and rows of metal shelves under dim, flickering fluorescent lights. He took Melinda by the hand and led her all the way to the back, to a door with a red circle on it. He unlocked the door and pulled her inside, locking it behind them. They stood in a small room with a staircase in its center, winding down into the caverns beneath. He lit the lantern hanging at the top of the staircase. With the lantern in one hand and Melinda in the other, they descended the staircase and entered the door to the secret archive room.

Dr. Lawrence told Melinda all about his family's legacy to manage and protect the secret archive, and how one day it would become their child's responsibility. Melinda marveled at the priceless works of art and first edition literature. He pulled an engagement ring from his jacket pocket and began to get down on one knee, when he tipped over the lantern. It took a split second for the nearest object catch fire, and soon everything in the archive was ablaze. There wasn't time for Dr. Lawrence to save both Melinda and the materials he was sworn to protect. He began to usher Melinda out the door to safety, and at the last moment changed his mind. He turned around and headed back into the archive, just as the doorway collapsed. He was pinned in the middle, with exactly one half of his body held within the flames. Melinda ascended the staircase into the basement of the library and pulled the fire alarm, causing the sprinkler system to engage, and fled from the building. Melinda was devastated by his choice. She left the school and never spoke to him again.

We were able to drive onto campus, park in the faculty lot, and walk right into the English department building without any interruptions. The door to the faculty offices was open, but Dr. Lawrence's office door was locked. Sarah pulled a bobby pin from her hair and picked the lock with a disturbing amount of ease.

While Sarah grabbed the first edition from the desk and tucked it inside her jacket, I went straight to the bookcase and removed the same row of red leather-bound volumes Dr. Lawrence had. I pushed the back of the empty panel until I felt it give way. I pulled out the cigar box and set it on the desk, leaning over it. Sarah leaned over the box as well, shining her phone's flashlight on it. I slid open the cover and reached my hand inside to pull out the stack of old letters. The office lights came on. Dr. Lawrence stood in the open doorway, clearing his throat.

"I believe I mentioned those letters were to remain in my office, Miss Farmer. And you, Sarah…" he shook his head in disappointment.

"Hi, Dad."

Eliza's Manuscript

I was almost out of time. Margaret Fuller's guest lecture at the university was just a few weeks away. She informed me that her agent would be with her, and she would be expecting a completed manuscript for her review. I still hadn't been able to write a single word of my own. I had incredible concepts. I had more than enough research. I had extensive notes. But any time I sat down with the intent to start writing, my mind was as blank as the page. Everything I wanted to say, every story I wanted to tell, was trapped inside of my mind.

Every time Margaret checked in, I told her things were going well. *Lie.* There was no way I was going embarrass myself by having nothing when they arrived. It needed to be done, and it needed to be good. Better than good. I would never get another chance like this. There was a manuscript somewhere on this property, I knew it, and I needed it. Unknown first-time authors don't get the attention of high-powered agents. They don't have the personal cell phone number of Pulitzer prize-winning, best-selling authors. I had both. This was my one big break, and I was not going to blow it.

I tore apart the study. I checked every single book for notes, inscriptions, and hidden compartments. I ran my hands over every square inch of the bookcases, looking for secret panels like the one in Dr. Lawrence's office. I went back to Eliza's bedroom, pushed the desk aside, and removed the floorboards. Her secret hiding place was empty. I returned to the cottage and checked everything there a second time as well. Nothing, except more poison oak.

I yelled into the quiet, empty rooms of the house, at Eliza, wherever she was. "If you want your book finished, then tell me where it is!" I hoped to God she hadn't been buried with it. Though it was certainly a last resort, I convinced myself that if Eliza had the chance to publish her book, and all she needed to do was dig up Ethan's body, she would swallow her fears and get the job done. Not the spiders or the snakes, or even Ethan's ghost, could stop her. I was more than a little irritated. Why did I always have to work so hard, and go to such great lengths, for the things I wanted? It never seemed to be enough to be *willing* to do anything, I actually had to *do* whatever it took. The dirty work, the sacrifice, the torment, was always on me. I had to lose Amy in order to be with Adam. I had to postpone my education so Adam could gain his. To be a writer, I had to sell everything and leave the city behind. To have the house, I had to live within its constraints, and with Eliza skulking about. I deserved a win. A big one.

I heard Adam's Jeep coming up the driveway. I looked out the front parlor window, the floor creaking beneath me as it always did, and once again imagined that Eliza was beneath it, clawing at the underside of the floorboards, trying desperately to reach me. I had a thought. I pulled back the antique area rug to find a small section of the floorboards had been cut away and replaced. That evening, once Adam went to sleep, I returned to the same spot in the parlor floor with a hammer and a crowbar. I began prying up the floorboards as quickly and quietly as I could. There, in a small, shallow grave beneath the floorboards, wrapped in parchment paper and again in heavy cloth, then raveled in petrified suede cording, was Eliza's unfinished manuscript. The musty smell of old cedarwood consumed the air around me as I carefully unwrapped my saving grace.

It was written longhand, in cursive, on individual sheets of journal paper, with crude sketches in many of the margins. This was not only what she wrote in the cottage following Ethan's death, this was the sum of everything Eliza had ever written. When Eliza passed away, Jenny must have gathered it from the cottage, ordered and bound it, and hidden it here where it would be protected until it could one day be discovered by the right person. Perhaps she had even hidden it here for me specifically, and then called me here to find it once I had the right connections established in the publishing world. There had not been a writer in the family since Eliza. She had obviously been waiting for me. Jenny could speak to the dead as well as see the future, she must have had a strong hand in orchestrating all of this.

It took every hour of every day I had left to scan each handwritten page into a live text software program and compile it into a formatted document. Eliza's handwriting was so frantic at times, the program couldn't interpret all of her words, so I typed those sections manually. I poured over the document dozens of times, repairing and updating the language. It was a remarkable piece of work. Eliza was brilliant, though it was evident her

107

insanity spiraled deeper with each chapter. She was an incredible writer. I would not have hesitated to place her in the company of some of the greatest early American authors of all time.

All it needed was an ending.

I told myself that it was really just an imaginative retelling of a story that's been told a thousand times before, though Eliza might have actually been nearly the first to tell it. I told myself I had done so much work to bring the manuscript up to date, that I practically wrote it anyway. I told myself that it would be a literary injustice to put her now finished book back in its shallow grave beneath the floorboards and not share it with the world. I told myself whatever I needed to hear to convince myself it was acceptable to finish Eliza's book and hand it over to Margaret Fuller and her agent as my own. Nobody else would ever have to know.

The ending I gave it was a logical and timeless one. Finally, something that was easy to write. I'd come to know Eliza so well, we practically felt like the same person. Perhaps this was why I had never been able to write a single word of my own. I was meant to learn everything I could about Eliza, her family, and her home, so I would be equipped to pick up where she left off. I was meant to find Eliza's manuscript, finish it, and deliver it to the world for her. I was meant to be the voice she never had. It had to be why everything happened the way it did. It had to be why I was really brought to Haven. It felt so empowering, to finally be in control of something, to finally be working on something that truly mattered. I took Eliza's lack of interference as validation that this was what she wanted from me all along, to find her book and to finish it. Unlike the many who tried, and failed, to complete Jane Austen's final manuscript, I was equal to the task. Possibly even born for it.

I was riveted by Margaret Fuller's guest lecture at Kingston University. It was truly captivating. She focused on the topic of crime and injustice in early American history, and how it fueled the supernatural subject matter of classic American literature. In a time when we knew so little about human nature and the world around us, the supernatural became a comforting way to explain away the intense and often senseless tragedies of everyday life, with a belief in forces well beyond our understanding or control. Despite significant scientific and technological advancements as a society over the past two hundred years, we certainly hadn't evolved much as human beings, especially when it came to placing blame or accepting culpability for our actions.

Following a brief question and answer period and a book signing in the lobby outside the auditorium, Margaret introduced me to her literary agent, Barbara Saxon. We went to dinner in South Haven, at a small upscale restaurant located inside a beautiful historic inn. South Haven was often a stopping point for people traveling up the peninsula to the small, seasonal tourist towns along the rise. There wasn't much more to it than the university, a few lodging and dining options, and a gas station. Following dinner and conversation, I presented them with my completed manuscript.

American Gothic by Elizabeth Farmer

I did my best to push down the nauseous feeling that washed over me the second the manuscript left my hands for theirs. This night was too important to me. I wanted to stay as long as they'd have me, and absorb every moment I had with the both of them. I'd been waiting years for this. I had come so far, and gone through so much, to get to this. I deserved this. My right leg was shaking uncontrollably underneath the table. I discreetly peeked down at my phone to check for any missed calls or texts from Adam every so often. Something didn't feel right.

The drive back to Haven was a short one, but it seemed so much longer that night. I sped down Haven Hill Road, past the old cemetery, and pulled onto the long, winding blacktop driveway leading to the house. Just then, the trees opened up like a dramatic theater curtain, revealing the glorious white gothic farmhouse at the top of the hill.

There it was.

Rotting. Crumbling. Leaning. Smoke billowing out from the doors and windows. I sprang from my car and ran through the porch door into the kitchen, to the worst stench I have ever smelled, like burning garbage. The walls were covered with scorch marks and the air was filled with thick, black smoke. I ran through the house, calling to Adam.

"Adam, are you here? Adam?! We have to get out of the house!"

I got turned around a number of times on my way through the house, trying to find Adam. The layout had completely changed, and it suddenly looked as if it had been deteriorating for decades. Everything was warped, water damaged and stained. The floors were rotten and sloped, bowing and splitting under my feet. The walls were cracking and crumbling, the ceilings were falling down around me. The windows shattered and the doors fell of their hinges, one by one, just as I ran past them. All of the beautiful furnishings were broken and covered with dirt and debris.

Adam wasn't here, but Eliza was. She was sitting up straight on her bed, facing the door to the hall as I ran past, her hands clasped neatly in front of her, clutching her spice tin of crooked nails. She stood up and followed me through the house as I desperately tried to find my way out. The whole house shook. The stairs gave way beneath my feet, causing me to tumble down the last few steps and land at the bottom, twisting my ankle. The paint began to bubble and peel. The artwork fell down and crashed to the floor, leaving a blanket of broken glass in my path and a sizeable shard embedded in my left thigh. Eliza stood at a distance, quietly watching as I panicked and cried.

I needed to get the first editions out, if I could manage it before the house claimed me. Why would I let them be destroyed too, when so much good could come from saving them? The house shifted again, just as I reached the study. I lost my balance. My upper body banged into the door frame, and a large splinter of wood sliced down the length of my right arm. All of the books fell from the bookshelves into a huge pile on the floor. Eliza's way of preventing me from taking her books, I assumed. I began sifting through them as quickly as I could, until I had all of the first editions stuffed into my book bag. I slung the heavy bag over my shoulder and grabbed my jade plant from the corner of the gorgeous antique desk, just as its legs turned inward and it collapsed upon itself.

The wrap-around porch came down right behind me as I fled the house and ran across the driveway to my car. The blacktop was melting, and I felt myself sinking into the ground as it rose up and claimed the soles of my shoes. I looked back at the house as I tossed my book bag across the driver's seat onto the passenger side. The house was completely dilapidated and covered in dead overgrowth. Eliza was standing in the front parlor window, looking out at me from her favorite spot. I sped down the driveway, praying that if I moved fast enough, the blacktop wouldn't consume my car and me along with it. I didn't dare look behind me. I knew as soon as I reached the main road, and was off the property, I would be safe again. It seemed to take an eternity to get there.

Adam wasn't angry that I took the first editions, or the manuscript. In his mind, we bought the property and all its contents, and they were ours. He was understandably disappointed that I hadn't been honest with him about anything I'd been going through since we arrived in Haven. He reminded me that we were a team, and if we weren't going to navigate this life together, then what was the point? As far as what happened to the house, he had no trouble believing what the police and fire department had determined. The peninsula had a series of fault lines running beneath it, created long ago by icebergs passing below. Every now and then, the Earth's plates experience a shift, wreaking havoc on whatever lies above. I pretended I believed it too.

Sarah invited us to stay in the small apartment above the metaphysical shop for as long as we needed to. Barbara Saxon called first thing in the morning. She read the manuscript on her way back to the city, and she loved it.

"This is absolutely brilliant," she professed. "It's a best-seller. There's no doubt in my mind."

I told Barbara the truth of the manuscript's origin and completion. I didn't have to, but I wanted to. It was the right thing to do. I asked her to please change the accreditation to:

American Gothic by Eliza Jane Rowe, with Elizabeth Farmer

Barbara was thrilled. She seemed to think this would make the book, and me as an author, even more marketable. She said the intrigue of an author finding a 150-year-old manuscript in her new home and choosing to work with it would sell thousands of copies, and spark dozens of articles and interviews. Sarah seemed to think it would please Eliza as well. She would finally be a published author. She deserved the credit for her hard work, and I deserved credit for the assist. Margaret Fuller insisted on writing the foreword, since none of this would have happened without her advice.

I wrote a book all my own during the months we stayed in the small apartment above Sarah's shop. We were living in tighter quarters than ever, but we had everything we needed, and everything had its place. This time, I took a much simpler approach to the writing process: Start writing. Keep writing. Finish writing. The manuscript came together quickly and effortlessly. Sometimes I would pretend we had taken the small apartment above the metaphysical shop the first day we arrived in Haven, and that my whole experience with the Rowe farm had just been a bad dream that fueled a good story.

When the book was complete, I carefully slid the thick bundle of bound pages into a manila envelope addressed to Barbara Saxon, tore back the adhesive seal, and pressed down the closure. We climbed into Adam's Jeep, packed with what little we still had. On my lap was my cherished jade plant and the manila envelope containing my completed manuscript. We delivered our keys for the Rowe farm to the Haven Historical Society, who would be spearheading its renovation and transformation into a museum and nature preserve, using the funds from the sale of another first edition. *American Gothic* was indeed a best-seller, and I used half of its profits to establish the Haven Paranormal Research Foundation, placing Sarah at the helm. It was going to do wonders for tourism.

It was a done deal.

I dropped the manila envelope in the mailbox outside the library on our way back to the Jeep. Just a few minutes later, we pulled into the driveway of our newly constructed seaside home, which we designed together with the help of my sister, Kate. It was elegant in its simplicity, with more windows than walls, to capitalize on the incredible views. It was a contemporary and wide-open space, without a single hiding place for secrets. Complete transparency, from here on out.

We took a walk along the beach. Adam doted on me as I waddled my way through the sand, my hands cradling my very pregnant stomach, and we talked about the future. He was lobbying hard to deliver the baby himself, and I was listing all the reasons why we should adopt a dog. It was a beautiful, clear afternoon, not a cloud in the sky. It still looked and felt like summer, but the scent of the air told me that fall was just around the corner. Fall was my favorite season. Sweaters, boots, falling leaves, and pumpkin spice everything.

It was a homecoming.

That night, I sat down in my new writing room for the first time, and began my next novel. The walls were painted a soothing blue-green color called tidewater, and they were lined with crisp white bookshelves filled with books, family photos, sculptural pieces of driftwood, and bowls heaping with stones and beach glass we'd been collecting together on our daily walks. We promised one another we'd make everything in this house very personal and meaningful to us. On the corner of my desk was, of course, my cherished jade plant. How this plant was still alive and well, I would never understand.

In the distance, at the top of Haven Hill, I could see the Rowe house and observe its renovation. Every so often, just long enough for me to notice, the lights would come on all at once. Eliza's way of saying hello, and letting me know that all was well. Later that fall, we welcomed a son. We named him Rowe.

We finally had it all.

American Gothic

Nearly five years had passed since Katherine Farmer last saw her sister, Elizabeth. She took a few days off from running her father's construction company to make the trip from Essex, Connecticut to the charming little seaside town of Haven, located on New York's northernmost peninsula, a few hours northeast of New York City. She used the quiet time on the drive to prepare and rehearse the best answer she could come up with as to why it had taken her this long to visit. Really, there was no acceptable excuse. Haven was charming and quaint. Hauntingly beautiful. It was a little bit like a ghost town, quiet and still, with an eerie whistle to the wind that glided inland over the water's surface. Kate pulled off to the side of the road, got out of her car, and began taking pictures of the incredible architecture and the amazing views. It inspired her, and it'd been a while since anything had inspired her. Staring out at the beautifully blue water, she fantasized about moving to Haven and building a new life for herself. She imagined rediscovering the close relationship she used to have with her sister. She envisioned finding meaningful work designing unique homes that respectfully communed with the local landscape. Meeting a smart, kind, and good-looking man would round out a pretty fulfilling new life in Haven. A rare trifecta.

It was almost time to see her. Kate drove slowly down Haven Hill Road, past the old cemetery, watching the lot markers for the right lot code. She pulled onto the long, winding blacktop driveway marked with the lot code HHS-1111. Just then, the trees opened up like a dramatic theater curtain, revealing a glorious white gothic farmhouse at the top of the hill.

There it was.

Haven Hill Sanitarium. It was meticulously maintained, and the ornate detailing was exquisite. It was a goddess of wood and stone. A place to be worshipped. Whoever designed it, she thought, was a genius well ahead of their time. She took a few more photos on her way to the front entrance, to text to her father. This was the Holy Grail of houses, with one of everything, just like they'd always talked about finding one day. Inside, every large, bright space was perfectly appointed, but completely impersonal, just as you'd expect from an institution of this kind.

Kate did her best to push down her overwhelming anxiety. She had no idea if Elizabeth would be happy to see her, or even want to see her. Mr. Farmer had never come to visit. Mrs. Farmer visited weekly at first, then monthly, then not at all.

"Good morning," she said to the woman behind the front desk. "Katherine Farmer to see Dr. Shepherd."

"Of course, Miss Farmer. Please have a seat in the parlor and I'll let Dr. Shepherd know you're here."

Kate sat in the chair beneath the front parlor window, noting the creak in the floorboards as she sat. She laughed to herself, thinking that if her mother had been here, she'd likely make a crack about her weight causing the floor to bow. She looked out the window, imagining all the people who had looked out this window before her, and how their views must have differed from her own.

"Dr. Shepherd will see you now."

The nurse showed her to the study. She admired the hand-crafted bookcases, full of interesting old books that looked to be arranged very specifically. What a handsome office this was, overlooking the beautiful flower gardens. Kate noticed the doctor was quite handsome as well. His eyes were so beautifully blue.

"Good morning," he started as he entered the room, reaching out his hand to shake hers. "Thank you so much for coming. How was your drive?"

Kate mentioned how beautiful the changing leaves were along the trip. Fall had always been her favorite season. Sweaters, boots, falling leaves, and pumpkin spice everything.

It was a homecoming.

"As I mentioned over the phone, Dr. Whitmore recently retired. I relocated here to take his place, and I'm still in the process of bringing myself up to speed on our current residents. I've been searching high and low since I arrived, and strangely, I haven't been able to locate Elizabeth's case file. So I searched the statewide records database…" He pulled a stack of printouts from his desk drawer and fanned them out on the desktop. "I was not expecting what I found." It'd been a long time since Kate had seen all the terrible things that were written about her sister. She chose to keep looking forward at the handsome doctor instead.

"Forgive me, but you seem very young to be the head of a psychiatric hospital."

Dr. Shepherd let out a small chuckle. "I think I was probably the only one willing to take the position. Not only is it a rather undesirable line of work, but we're terribly under-funded, and this area has become quite desolate, even dangerous, in recent years."

"I noticed that when I came through town," Kate commented. "What happened here?"

"The peninsula has a series of fault lines running beneath it, created long ago by icebergs passing below. Every now and then, the Earth's plates experience a shift, wreaking havoc on whatever lies above. That tends to put a damper on the local economy. The last shift was a pretty rough one, I'm told. Most of the residents left at that point."

The nurse entered the study carrying a tray with two cups of coffee and a tin of freshly baked chocolate chip cookies. "Thank you, Mary," he said kindly. "Mary here will be leaving us soon, too. She's retiring and moving to Florida. I don't know what we'll do without her."

"Florida sounds nice," Kate replied kindly.

"My daughter lives in St. Augustine. She's divorced now, so as soon as we can find a suitable replacement, I'll be heading down there to live with her and help with my grandbabies." Mary smiled as she backed out of the room and closed the door behind her.

"You're not looking for a job, are you? I'm having trouble getting anyone remotely qualified to even come this far north for an interview."

"I'm an architect, actually. I run my father's construction company in Connecticut."

"Oh nice, I love architecture. Do you enjoy it?"

"To be honest, no. Mass producing subdivision homes with no charm or discerning character is not at all what I saw myself doing with my degree. But everything that happened with Elizabeth nearly destroyed our family, so there was really no other option for me but to move home and help out."

"Would you mind telling me more about what happened with Elizabeth?"

"Of course. She was completely fine until her junior year of high school. Better than fine. Elizabeth was always beautiful, smart, and popular. She never had an awkward stage, an embarrassing moment, or so much as a bad hair day. It was truly unfair. She came to visit me at Columbia that summer. She was over the moon excited because the boy she'd been crushing on since middle school summer camp was being transferred to her school for their senior year.

The local Catholic high school was being shut down due to faltering attendance, and the students were being integrated with the public high school. Elizabeth was certain that fate was finally bringing them together.

The schools made a big deal of the homecoming football game that year, because it was the last time the public and parochial schools would ever play against each other. The Angels versus the Devils. The following year, they'd be part of the same team.

Elizabeth and her best friend, Amy, had an argument after the game. Amy wanted to get coffee and discuss books, like they always did, but Elizabeth wanted to hang around the school grounds and get a glimpse of her crush coming up from the locker room. His Jeep was still in the parking lot, so she assumed he hadn't yet left the school. Amy walked home alone, cutting through the park across the street from the high school to get there faster. She was approached by a few players from the opposing team, who were hanging out in the park, drinking. They cornered her in the park pavilion, and they raped her. One of the boys covered her face with his jacket to keep her quiet, unintentionally suffocating her. That boy was Elizabeth's crush – the rival quarterback, Ethan Rowe. Amy had asthma…it took less than a minute for her to die. When they realized she was dead, they panicked, left her body there, and fled. Elizabeth saw the boys running back to the school parking lot, pile into the Jeep, and peel out. When she found out what had happened to Amy, she pieced it together. She went to the police with what she thought she knew, but it wasn't nearly definitive enough. The boys were never charged.

That was the start of everything.

After speaking to the police, she stopped speaking altogether. She dyed all of her clothes a dark gray, and altered them to cover her entire body. She stopped bathing and brushing her hair. When she started carrying a small tin of construction nails to school with her, the school board recommended home-based study. She started spending most of her time at the public library, obsessed with researching religion, spirituality, and the paranormal. She insisted that Amy's ghost was following her, tormenting her, blaming Elizabeth for what had happened to her.

One day she walked into the library to find Ethan and his friends there, seated at the table where she and Amy always sat. She claimed Amy was seated at the table, too. They immediately started teasing Elizabeth about how she looked. Ethan had no idea who she was. Something inside her snapped. She charged toward him, climbed right over the top of the table, and plunged a construction nail into his neck. Ethan bled out on the library floor, right beneath the glass case of priceless first editions."

"My God."

"The Rowe family eventually agreed in court to institutionalization over incarceration, as long as she was permanently kept at a safe distance. They were concerned for the safety and well-being of Ethan's younger sister. Has she spoken at all, since she's been here?"

"No, she hasn't, but she's present. She's always observing. Always thinking. You can see it in her eyes. I'd love to know what's going on inside her mind. She writes a great deal, but destroys most of it. What I've managed to see of it is just repetitive nonsense.

Mary tells me all used to be peaceful. My arrival here seems to have stirred something within her. She glides around the building day and night like a ghost; we can't seem to keep her in, or out, of anywhere. She moves the furniture, only to put it right back where it was. She constantly rearranges the bookshelves in my office; it looks to be arranged very specifically, but it's not a system we can make any sense of. When I arrive in the morning, there is often a blank Word document opened on my computer screen. Mary thought, perhaps if we could lure a member of her family here, you might help us determine how we can appease her."

Dr. Shepherd escorted Kate through the first-floor common rooms, toward the staircase leading to the patient rooms. Each room was tastefully and minimally furnished with simple, classic pieces and calming neutral tones. Everything was spotless and perfectly placed. There was nothing to distract from all the amazing details. Original hardwoods throughout. Vaulted ceilings. Original cabinetry, all built by hand. Lots of built-ins. Wainscoting. Crown molding. As an architect, she couldn't help but admire it.

"This building is quite incredible," she commented.

"Isn't it? This was a very prosperous farm at one time, I'm told. The only one on the entire northernmost peninsula. It was originally built in the late 1800s by John Freeman, a former slave, and his wife, Jenny, who the townspeople believed to be a witch."

A patient clinging to the wall at the top of the stairs smiled at Kate and stretched out her bony, ring-covered hand to her just as they reached the second floor. A black tattoo peeked out from the bell sleeve of her white peasant top.

"You're going to need a friend like me," she whispered through her chilling grin, and laughed.

"Please go back to your room, Sarah," Dr. Shepherd said sternly. "I'm sorry about that."

They continued through the maze of hallways lined with closed doors. Corridors got darker and narrower just before you entered expansive, light-filled spaces, creating a feeling of compression and release that left you physically disoriented. Doors led to other doors, which led to angular, awkward spaces, and sharp turns resulted in abrupt stopping points. This building makes a perfect sanitarium, Kate thought to herself. If you weren't already mad when you arrived, this place could quickly drive you to it.

There was a man seated in an armchair on the right side of the hallway, next to a small table with a lamp on it, reading a book. He looked quite normal as they approached him, but as they passed by, Kate was startled by his gruesome left side. He was bald with purplish red, rippled skin. His left ear was completely melted shut and his partially-open left eye was a cloudy white. His reddish-brown hair and beard stopped precisely in the center of him, as if half of a man and half of a demon had been fused together.

"Good morning, Professor Lawrence," Dr. Shepherd smiled.

"She's cleaning my office," he said, nodding in the direction of his open room, where Mary was inside making the bed. "Please remind her those letters are to remain in my office."

"I'll do that, Professor. Have a good day." Professor Lawrence nodded again and returned to his book.

"Professor Lawrence lost his wife several years ago," Dr. Shepherd filled Kate in quietly as they continued on. "She was a former student of his. He believes he came home from the university to find his house ablaze and collapsing, and that he barely made it out alive trying to save her life. The truth of the matter is, he came home to find his wife was having an affair. Dr. Lawrence set the fire himself, and sustained burns over half of his body while making sure both she and her lover did not make it out alive. All he has left of her is a stack of love letters she'd written to him in college. He treasures them. He often believes his room here is his former office in the English department at the university.

As I've brought myself up to speed on each of the patients here, I've learned that most have created an alternate reality in order to absolve themselves from something terrible they've done. Here we are."

Dr. Shepherd gently knocked on Elizabeth's door before opening it. She was sitting on the edge of the bed, her hands clasped neatly in front of her, looking out the window. Her dark gray dress covered her entire body, and her hair was pulled back into a tight bun. A jade plant sat on the corner of the desk. Her room smelled like urine. A patient in the next room was incessantly banging on their shared wall. Elizabeth turned to face the doorway, having no reaction to seeing her sister standing there. Her chest, neck, and wrists were covered in some kind of rash. As she rubbed at her inflamed skin, it became more irritated.

"Good morning, Elizabeth. You have a visitor," Dr. Shepherd smiled as he ushered Kate into the room.

"Hey Betsy…it's Kate…how are you?" Kate moved cautiously toward the bed and sat down beside her, but Elizabeth kept her eyes locked on Dr. Shepherd, who still stood there, leaning against the door frame. "Mom and Dad send their love. I brought your favorite book from home. *American Gothic* by Margaret Fuller." Elizabeth had read it at least a dozen times. "I remember the day you and Amy went to that bookstore in the city before sunrise to be first in line for her signing…"

"That's a great book," Dr. Shepherd interjected. "I've read it at least a dozen times."

"Really?" Kate rose from her seat next to Elizabeth and walked back to Dr. Shepherd. "Betsy always wanted me to read it. I'm not much of a reader, but maybe you could tell me about it."

"I'd be happy to. Are you staying in town tonight, would you like to have dinner with me? I hope that's not too forward. There's a shortage of good company around here. I'm dying for a great conversation." A large, dry lump formed in Elizabeth's throat upon hearing those words.

"Not at all. I'd love that," Kate said casually, while screaming on the inside.

"Oh great, where are you staying?"

"I'm staying at a beautiful historic inn, in South Haven, by the university."

"Perfect, they have a fantastic restaurant there..."

Elizabeth discreetly slid her shoe over the nail hole in the floorboard next to her bed, as she watched Kate and Dr. Shepherd together. A drop of blood fell onto the bosom of her simple gray dress as she tightened her grip on the crooked nail hiding within her fist.